THE DEMETER FLOWER

THE DEMETER FLOWER

ROCHELLE SINGER

ST. MARTIN'S PRESS,
NEW YORK

DESIGNED BY MANUELA PAUL

Library of Congress Cataloging in Publication Data

Singer, Rochelle.
  The Demeter flower.

  I. Title.
PZ4.S61812De [PS3569.I565] 813'.54 80 –14015
ISBN 0 –312–19194–4

To
Laurie

THE DEMETER FLOWER

I walked into the party alone, responding as cheerfully as I could to friendly calls of "Hi, Morgan." I wasn't feeling particularly cheerful. Sunny and I had argued at dinner, bickering over the petty household things you fight about with a lover when there's something wrong with the love between you. I wasn't sure, but I thought I had started it by frowning at a cracked cup. Then, before we'd had a chance to make up, she'd gone off to discuss some village business with our chief carpenter. I expected she'd show up in a while, here at Luna's house.

I looked around me, searching for someone to spend time with. I saw Calliope, my closest friend, standing at the other end of the room. She saw me too, we waved to each other, and I wriggled my way through the clusters of laughing, talking women.

Luna's party was a double celebration. It had been

planned for her twenty-sixth birthday, but earlier that week another reason had been announced: Calliope had decided to have a daughter. She had chosen her flower; the leaves were being dried, and that morning as each of us hurried to our work, she had told me the ceremony would take place in about six weeks, mid-month after the next games. I questioned her teasingly now, my arm around her plump shoulders.

"A Demeter feast? Calliope, nobody does that any more."

She shrugged. "What do I care what anybody does?" She was smiling, but her dark eyes were serious. "As far as I'm concerned, a lot of people are doing a lot of dumb things." She glanced at Luna on the other side of the room. "Did you know that not one founder was invited to this party?"

I nodded. My mother had mentioned it to me. "I think Diana was hurt."

"Yes, well, she does love parties." Calliope laughed. She knew my mother as well as I did. She had been a small child when her own mother died in a logging accident, and she had spent a lot of growing-up time with us. "Everybody will be invited to mine." She poured herself a glass of beer from the pitcher on the table. "This beer is terrible. My science students made it."

I tasted some of the pale yellow liquid in her cup. It was thin and sour. "I hope they didn't make very much of it," I said. "What are you going to do anyway? A whole elaborate ceremony?"

"No. Nothing formal. A picnic in the woods. Music, dancing, food, wine—I don't think we'll have any beer." She put her cup down on the table, half full, and looked at it with distaste.

"You're not going to march around the playing field or parade through the center of town carrying a sheaf of wheat?" We both laughed. Some of our least favorite people had staged some of the most elaborate rituals the village had ever seen.

"I can't. The wheat won't be ripe," she said with a straight face. Then, mischievously, "Maybe just a little ceremony when I drink the tea. You know, a round of applause for one more little black baby coming to town."

"How does Ocean feel about all this?"

"She likes the idea of helping with a child, but she teases me about the ceremony. She says she won't come. I think she's joking."

"Where is Ocean, anyway?" I was suddenly aware of her absence.

Calliope nodded toward the kitchen. "With the birthday cake. Luna asked her to bake it."

I raised an eyebrow. "They're not exactly close friends."

Calliope shrugged. "Well, she does bake good cakes."

The crowd stirred and parted near the kitchen door. Ocean appeared, the twenty-six flaming candles held well away from her chest, and headed for the crowded table. Luna hovered near her shoulder, waiting for her to set the cake down. Calliope and I moved closer in time to hear Luna say urgently to the hesitating Ocean, "The candles are melting." Calliope put the beer pitcher on the floor, and Luna put the cake where the pitcher had been.

Luna, eyes closed and mouth twisted with concentration, made her wish, took a deep breath, and blew out all the candles at once, opening her eyes as she blew. She accepted the congratulations of those standing near her graciously, smiling slightly and nodding.

"It isn't actually the force of the breath that does it, you know," she began, crossing her arms over her stocky torso. "It has more to do with the evenness of the air flow and the consistency of the force . . ."

Calliope groaned and led me to the other side of the room, near the outside door. "Want to go for a walk? I'm

3

afraid she'll start singing next." I nodded. Luna fancied herself a composer and at parties would often take out the old guitar her mother had brought to Demeter and begin to sing some of what Calliope called her "pale moon" music.

But just as we were about to move outside the door, a slender young woman with dark blond hair and an energetic stride came in the door, shouted "Calliope!" and swept my friend up in her arms, nearly lifting her off the floor. She hugged her and kissed her on both cheeks before she turned to me, gave me a brief embrace, and asked if I didn't think it was "wonderful about Calliope." I smiled and agreed that it was.

"And we'll be birthing within a couple of months of each other," Athena added brightly, turning again to Calliope. "But why are you waiting six weeks?"

"I thought winter would be a nice time to be big and uncomfortable."

"Amazing," Athena said. "You've got it all planned. I just decided to do it and went ahead and did it."

"That's right," I said, smirking at Calliope. "And you didn't even have a ceremony."

Calliope punched me lightly on the arm and told Athena, "She thinks I'm an exhibitionist." I was protesting, laughing, when Luna approached us and spoke directly to me.

"Where's Sunny, Morgan?" I was used to Luna's peremptory attitude and didn't mind it. Calliope usually allowed herself to be amused by it. But Athena, younger than we were and less tolerant of rudeness, sighed loudly, excused herself, and went to talk to another friend.

"She'll be here in a while. She's talking to Sara about some designs for the school addition."

"Oh. Well, it probably won't be necessary to do any building right now. Sunny can save her designs for the new village." There it was again, Luna and her new village. Even

4

as an adolescent, Luna had been an organizer, and for years she'd been talking about leaving Demeter and starting a second village. "Expansion," she called it. Few of us had ever taken her talk very seriously.

"What's Sunny got to do with it?" I retorted as coolly as I could. Luna had an irritating I-know-something-you-don't-know expression on her sallow face. She raised her thin black eyebrows and shrugged.

"Sounds like you're really planning to leave," Calliope said, looking nervously from Luna to me and back to Luna again. Calliope could deal with a real argument as well as the next woman, but this innuendo was making her uncomfortable.

"Of course we are. More and more women are becoming convinced that they should consider becoming part of our movement. They don't want to sit here and stagnate for the rest of their lives." I had begun to settle into the stupor I reserved for Luna's speeches when her next statement shocked me back to life. "I for one want to do something important before I get as old and boring as the women who founded this place."

"Boring!" I shouted at her. "They're vital, strong, brave—they built this place and gave birth to us and made Demeter a good place for us to grow up in!"

My shouting had attracted some attention. Luna spoke softly. "Yes, well, I've grown up now. And they're still running it. They're still trying to tell us what to do and when to do it."

"That's ridiculous," Calliope said shortly. "We have the same voice they do. There are daughters on the council —including you, Luna."

Luna shrugged again. "Let's not talk about it. This is a party." She looked at our glasses. "How can you drink that awful beer? There's juice and wine in the kitchen. If you see Sunny before I do, tell her I'm looking for her, will you?" She went off to circulate among her guests, leaving the two of us staring at each other, angry and perplexed.

Calliope shook her head. "This party is beginning to depress me. Let's take our walk."

"Let's."

We walked in silence for a while. I was thinking about what Luna had said. Our village was forty years old, and I suppose there were those who found its challenges less than exciting. But most of us who were not close to Luna and her plans thought the idea of a new village a romantic dream, a game devised by women who saw themselves as sophisticated, daring, and adventurous. Personally, I didn't see the point at all, unless the point was nothing more than Luna's restless, dissatisfied personality.

Luna was a drifter even within the limits of the village. She never settled on any job for long, and even though most of us did a variety of work, we still had primary interests and primary jobs. She didn't. My mother called her a "politician," and I thought the term was a charitable one.

My primary job, I felt, gave me a special understanding of the village. I was the chronicler, the recorder of our history. I knew very well what we had accomplished in these forty years and what still had to be done. We had new fields to cultivate, improvements to make in our power systems, new methods to discover of teaching our young. Even though we had nearly tripled our original population, I didn't feel we were strong enough, sure enough, to think of splitting off from the mother village, taking a chunk of the unfinished whole, and moving it off to a new place.

Where the pear orchard opened onto the playing field, Calliope and I stopped and sat down on a dead tree that served as a spectators' bench for the games. My friend, too, had been thinking of our conversation with Luna.

"Is Sunny really involved in this new settlement?" she asked me suddenly.

"I don't know. I know she's talked to Luna about it, but she hasn't said much to me."

6

"What if she wants to go?"

I picked a twig up off the ground and began to peel the bark away. Calliope waited quietly for my answer.

"I don't know. She's been kind of strange lately. We don't talk very much. If you'd asked me that a few months ago, I would have said, 'if she goes, I go.' Now I'm not sure any more. Sometimes the house feels crowded when we're there together. I don't know how to explain it." Calliope nodded and said nothing, waiting for me to go on. "She's just different, restless, like there's something else she'd rather be doing. And I feel different, too, not like myself at all. One day I feel old and stodgy—when Luna was talking in there tonight, about the elders being boring, I felt as if she were talking about me—and other times, I feel like being completely irresponsible, crazy, flirting, playing, just dropping the load I feel like I'm carrying the rest of the time."

"You feel wild sometimes, like tearing things apart?"

I nodded. "Like tearing Sunny and me apart. It's because of the way she is now."

"Sounds like the way I felt a couple of years ago."

"I remember."

"I did what I felt like doing. Not right away; I waited and waited until I couldn't wait any more, couldn't try to talk any more, and that was the end of it. And the end brought me to where I am now. Not so bad." She paused, then ruffled my hair lightly. "Listen, if you want to do something wild, what are you hanging around me for? There's a whole crowd of women at that party."

"When I'm still living with Sunny? I don't want to. And who'd want to get involved with me, anyway? Besides, there's nobody—"

"We were talking about playing, not about some big, serious thing."

I laughed. "I'm always serious. It's so depressing."

"And boring," Calliope said, laughing with me.

"You're as bad as I am. Well, maybe you'll work it out, you and Sunny." She stood. "Come on, let's go back to the party."

"No. I don't think so. I think I'll just walk some more and go home and go to bed."

"That's not the right choice. You're moping."

I shook my head. "No, I'm not. I just feel quiet. I want to be quiet, that's all."

I walked her back as far as Luna's house. The door was wide open. Sunny had arrived. I saw her talking animatedly to Luna and her friends, standing as she so often did, hands in her pockets, looking tall, rangy, beautiful, and happy. Happy as I hadn't seen her, in my company, for a while. Calliope looked at me quizzically. I shook my head. I didn't want to go back in. We hugged and said good night, and I walked off again, slowly, toward my own house.

It seemed odd to think of Calliope as a mother. I couldn't remember her ever being interested in creating anything but better windmills and sunlight collectors. She nurtured her generators, planning for their future. I began to think again—probably because I was feeling very lonely —about having a daughter myself, becoming part of the chain our founders began when they first brought the seeds of the yellow flower with them to Demeter. When Diana and Angel planted the seeds. When Angel dried the flower and brewed and drank the tea and gave birth to Firstborn. Within the first ten years, thirty women had daughters. In twenty years, there were more daughters and a dozen granddaughters.

Some women knew in their adolescence whether they wanted to have a child or two. Although I had passed thirty, I still wasn't sure. I didn't know how much I had to give, and while children were, in many ways, raised by the entire village, I knew there was a special relationship a child had to have with her mother if she was to grow up loving.

I felt like talking to Diana and began to walk toward her

house, although I didn't know what I wanted to say. I reached the playing field and looked across to the old farmhouse where she had lived with Angel since the founding. The lights were out. My mother and Angel had probably gone to bed. I stood looking at it for a moment, disappointed, and then turned again toward my own house.

Diana had been a good mother, always busy with her own projects but interested in mine, taking seriously my childish problems because she never forgot what it was like to be a child. Her strong memories of her own childhood, and the completely different world she grew up in, reinforced her determination to give me a sense of security in the world she had created. I was safe from the dangers and confusion she had faced; she could allow me to grow in my own way. She was appropriately relieved when I chose to move to the dormitory at age eight, pleased at my maturity when, at fourteen, I joined several other young women in our own house. She was tender and concerned when, at sixteen, my first love ended badly. I thought her wise, if apt sometimes to forget individuals—including me—in her concern for the group. But she was, after all, a founder. The village was her child, too, her work of art.

My house was dark. I walked quickly through the living room into the kitchen and lighted the lamp. The stove was still warm from dinner. I stirred up the fire, added some wood, and put on the kettle. I would have tea, read a little, and go to bed. That was my plan. I needed a plan, something I could follow step by step, keep in mind, keep beside me. I felt very lonely.

Two hours later, I was still reading, still alone, not sleepy, but tired. When I moved from my chair, I discovered that the muscles in my thighs and shoulders ached with tension. I had told myself that I was not waiting for Sunny, but my body told me it wasn't so. I went to bed and lay awake another hour before I heard the door open. I heard her walking quietly through the house. The bathroom door closed. I heard her pouring water from the pitcher into the old washbasin, splashing some on the floor, as always.

The bathroom door opened again, and the floor creaked as she walked through the kitchen to the bedroom.

"Are you awake?" she whispered.

"Yes." I had thought of pretending to be asleep, but decided that I probably couldn't pretend effectively enough.

"Why did you leave the party? You missed most of the fun."

"I guess I didn't feel like partying. I wanted to read."

"Oh. Okay." She sounded irritated. I felt her settle in beside me, searching for a sleeping position, sighing a little. Then she was still. I reached out. She was lying with her back to me. I touched her pale hair softly, trying to find her. She turned just enough to reach back and pat my hand lightly, not holding.

"Good night, Morgan."

"Good night." I pulled back, lying for a moment on my side, feeling the warmth of her body inches away. Then I moved farther away and turned on my stomach, the mattress cool against my breasts and thighs. I listened to her breathing. She was soon asleep. The bed had grown warm beneath me. I rolled over onto my back, looking out the window at the stark angles of the oaks against the sky. I thought of getting up, of going into the living room and reading until I could sleep, but my body was tired. I forced my breathing into a steady rhythm, closed my eyes, closed my mind, and eventually fell asleep.

Ocean, tending the goats, was the first to see them coming over the hill, the woman and the man. She saw the two small figures stop their horses just past the brow and look down into our valley. She had never seen a man before, except in pictures, so she couldn't be sure it was one from that distance. But it was enough that they were strangers. Leaving the goats, she alerted the village, racing down to the main street, seizing the first woman she met—Athena—and telling her to spread the word while Ocean gathered a party to bring the newcomers to the village.

I was working at the chronicle that morning. The building where we keep our history is in an out-of-the-way part of Demeter; buried in the storeroom, I remained unaware of the excitement until Athena rushed in the door to tell me. I was too stunned to speak until she touched my shoulder, her hand quivering with excitement.

"Strangers!" I said finally. This had never happened before. For some reason, it had never occurred to me that it might. And one of them a man.

"Yes, yes—that's right—come on!" She dragged me impatiently out the door and toward the main road. I could see them coming. I hesitated at the side of the road, watching, while Athena ran out to join the procession: four of our women on horseback, the two strangers on foot, Calliope in the lead, waving a spear and leading two horses I assumed belonged to the strangers, a dozen or more women bringing up the rear or walking beside the central figures, and three dogs, hysterical with snarling fear at the sight of the newcomers.

The woman appeared frail, although she was not small, and walked uncertainly, her shoulders hunched as if to conceal her breasts. The man was tall and muscular and walked proudly.

Calliope saw me approach. "He was carrying this," she shouted, brandishing the weapon. "It's a man." I knew it was a man. I made a wry face at her, and she smiled, embarrassed. But we were too frightened, too excited, to laugh at each other. "They were trying to get away, but we caught them. We're taking them to Diana."

I saw Sunny, close to the man, and even closer, another daughter of my generation, Freedom, strolling beside him and staring at him silently. As we walked, more women came out to look. Some backed away again when they saw the man; others moved closer to examine his strangeness.

I dropped back to walk with the strangers, encircled as they were by the band of women and gaped at by those who only watched them go by. Freedom was no longer staring at the man but had taken up her march close behind, looking as much at the woman as at the man.

"What are your names?" I asked.

Until I spoke, the man had been stalking grimly along, not looking at anyone. He turned to me. "My name is

Bennett," he said, an edge of anger in his voice. "Why have our horses been taken? Why are we being marched along this way?" The woman said nothing, but kept her eyes on the road just ahead of her feet.

"What's your name?" I repeated, this time to her alone. Still she didn't speak.

Bennett answered for her. "She's called Donna." He grabbed her arm and pulled her to a stop beside him. "We're not going any farther until you answer some of my questions." Ocean, walking just behind him with Freedom, surprised by the suddenness of his stop, bumped into him. Some of us laughed nervously. He didn't. "Where are you taking us? That's first."

"We're taking you to one of our elders," Calliope told him.

"A priest? Good. Where are the rest of your men?" He began walking again.

"We haven't any," I said. Although he stared at me when I said it, he kept on walking, still holding Donna's arm, pulling her along with him.

Diana, who had kitchen duty that day, was standing near the door of the dining hall, waiting. She had a spoon in her hand. A kitchen cat, frightened of the crowd, crouched behind her ankles. I saw her as a stranger would, tall, her long gray hair bound in a knot at the back of her head.

"Who is this?" Bennett asked me. He didn't wait for an answer, but pushed through the surrounding women and approached my mother. "Old woman, where are your men?"

Diana laid her spoon on a window ledge. "There are no men. I'm an elder, a mother. My name is Diana. Who are you?" She spoke in a flat, even tone. He didn't answer her immediately, but stood, hands on hips, looking around at the staring, whispering women. A few other elders had arrived, Sara, Joanna, Redwood, and Angel among them.

They neither whispered nor stared, but gazed at him coolly in an odd, detached way.

He turned back to Diana and, ignoring her question, demanded, "Why are there no men? And where is your priest, woman?"

She gazed at him, and although her look was speculative, I could see she was startled. "Priest?" she said softly, almost to herself. Sara, standing nearby, whispered something into Angel's ear. Angel nodded grimly. I remembered a vague reference to priests in the short, factual history of the founders' journey to Demeter.

The man was frowning fiercely at Diana, waiting for her answer. Instead, she turned a scowl at least as fierce on him. "I asked you a question, *man.*" Several elders laughed at her emphasis, but Sara and Joanna did not. Sara's fists were tight at her sides, her dark face flushed to a deeper brown by anger. Joanna was very pale.

Redwood stepped forward deliberately and took the spear from Calliope's hand. "Answer her question," she growled.

The man stared insolently at the tall, imposing woman, her face lined with years but her body firm and strong, her straight, white-streaked black hair plaited in a single long braid, her black eyes fixed on his, his own weapon in her hand. He didn't drop his eyes but he answered, "I'm Bennett. This is my woman, Donna."

"Good," Diana said. "And now I'll answer your questions. We have no priest, and there are no men because we chose to have none a long time ago. Donna?" She waited for the woman to answer. Donna looked up from her regard of a row of marigolds beside the door. "Why don't you speak?" Donna looked frightened. Sara, standing nearby, whispered something into Angel's ear, and Angel shook her head sadly. "Well, I'm sure you'll speak when you're ready to." Diana turned to Bennett. "We'll find work for both of you to do. Luna will find you a place to stay."

"We don't know that we will be staying," Bennett said quickly.

"We don't know that you'll be allowed to," Diana replied.

He flushed. "We'll do as we wish. We have a child coming, and—"

"You're pregnant?" Diana's question was sharp, and Donna stepped backward, nearly stumbling. "Well, I suppose it's to be expected."

"I don't think we'll want to stay here anyway," Bennett continued, as though he'd never been interrupted.

"I would like it best," Diana said wearily, "if you had never come. But you'll stay until we decide what to do."

"You can't make us stay here."

"I said you'll stay here," her voice was low and steady, "until we decide what to do. You'll be watched to make sure that you do stay. And you will not speak for Donna. Not here." She turned to Luna, standing nearby, feet wide apart, chin thrust forward aggressively. "Luna, help them get settled. Donna," she spoke gently to the woman, "please come to my house after dinner. Calliope will show you the way."

"Without me?" Bennett demanded.

"Yes. Without you."

Although all of us wanted to know about Donna, wanted to talk to her and ask her questions, Diana let it be known that the shy young woman should not be harassed by our curiosity, that she must not be frightened but welcomed quietly. She would be settled, given some task to occupy herself with, and left in peace. As for Bennett, we were even more curious about him—at least those of us who grew up in the village were—but we were, in turn, wary and shy of him. He seemed so strange to us. To approach him directly would be to acknowledge the fact of his presence, a fact that still seemed unbelievable to me. I was willing, for the time being, to leave the problem to Diana.

Nor did anyone else object seriously to her method, although Luna did some complaining at dinner.

"I think," she said, "it would make a great deal more sense if someone her own age talked to Donna. She might be more willing to let down her guard, tell about her life."

Freedom, who was sitting next to Luna at the large table, nodded her head, but said nothing. She had been quiet throughout the meal, glancing even more often than the rest of us toward the corner where Donna and Bennett sat. I attempted to involve her in our conversation and at the same time take it out of Luna's hands.

"I think Redwood scared him," I said to Freedom. "Your mother can be pretty ferocious."

Freedom shrugged, apparently less delighted with Redwood's performance than some of us had been. "My mother thinks that if you threaten a plow it will cut through rock."

Calliope, who admired Redwood's skill with tools and machines, pursed her lips disapprovingly and began to argue with Luna. "I don't see why it matters who talks to Donna—as long as it's someone who knows how to listen." Luna, the target of Calliope's sarcasm, glared at her but said nothing.

I was irritated with them both. "This whole conversation is stupid. Think what's happened. Think what we can learn. This is real. And we're arguing about who should talk to the woman first."

Luna smiled indulgently. "You and your sense of history. Reading about it, writing about it, *hearing* about it. That's not real."

"She acts funny, doesn't she?" Sunny made an attempt at changing the subject.

"Nervous," Freedom said. "Scared."

Ocean, silent and thoughtful until now, looked up from her food. "She makes herself look smaller than she is."

"And he makes himself look bigger," Calliope said. We all laughed, all but Freedom, who was once again contemplating Bennett. I followed her gaze to where he sat at a small table with Donna, Diana, Angel, Sara, and Joanna.

"He called her 'my woman,' " I said. "Like she's a goat or something."

"I'm sure he didn't mean it that way," Freedom said. "I think he's frightened, too."

I supposed she was right in a way, but I didn't think much about it. I was more interested in his behavior than in his motives.

My mother talked with Donna alone that night. It was a long talk, she told me later. The young woman had been reluctant to speak, but my mother's gentle insistence had reached her eventually, and she had told Diana about her life.

She was born on a farm somewhere far to the east of our village. She wasn't sure how far, only that she and Bennett had been traveling for about three months. She was eighteen years old. Before she had met Bennett, she had never been farther than the nearest village, a tiny market town a day's ride from her home. And she had been allowed to go there only a very few times, in the company of her entire family. She remembered clearly the day Bennett had arrived at the farm. Visitors were rare, and Bennett was a stranger, a terrifying sight—tall, golden-haired, handsome, and unknown.

Donna had just collected the eggs and was carrying them to the house when she heard the sound of hoofbeats. She had stopped, startled, her heart beating rapidly and hard. She had stood perfectly still in the doorway of her house, poised to run inside, holding the basket of eggs, staring at the horse and rider coming over the far crest of the road.

"Mother! A man is coming."

The old woman, her back bent and her face lined with

17

age—she was nearing fifty—came to the door to join her daughter and squinted toward the image she could barely see.

"Oh." She shook her head as if to clear it of preoccupation. "I thought they came just a while ago to collect. Better go and get your father." Donna knew that the priest's soldiers had already come for their yearly share of the farm's produce. This man was here for some other reason. She ran out to the far field where her father and three brothers were working to bring in the hay for winter feed. Her father was holding his hat in one hand, a shotgun in the other, looking in the direction of the horse and rider. The brothers were looking at each other in silent excitement.

"Mother says to come and get you, Father."

"I was coming. Jake, Billy, stay out here and keep a watch on the cows." The man turned toward the house, trailed by his youngest son, then by Donna.

"Is it a priest, Father?" the son asked.

"Doesn't look like one, does it?" the man growled. "Just some other kind of trouble." They reached the house just as the stranger was riding into the yard.

"Get in the house with your mother, Donna." She hesitated. "Now!" She glanced once again at the young man on the horse, then pushed open the door and went inside.

"Did you see the man, Mother?"

"I didn't see a man. And I don't want to." Her mother moved slowly toward the dim recess where the big iron stove squatted and began to build a cooking fire. Donna stood close to the window, afraid to pull back the curtain, listening to the conversation of the men.

"I heard there's some good land to the west, a hundred miles, maybe more," her father was saying.

"What's between here and there?"

"Not much."

"Any priest's villages?"

"Not that way, unless it's farther on. There's one south of here."

The young man hesitated. "I've been riding for a long time. I can pay for a few days' keep and some food to take with me when I go." He spoke pleasantly, easily, as though it didn't matter.

"What can you pay with?"

"I've got some small tools, some boots that might fit you, and I've got some pieces of gold and a little silver. And some jewels."

"Jewels?" Donna had heard the word before, but she'd never seen any. Her mother had told her about rings and bracelets and how jewels sparkled in the sun. She knew the priests and their men wore them sometimes, but she'd never been allowed to see such people. "I don't want any of that around—stolen jewels. You're a runaway, aren't you?" Her father's voice was hoarse with fear.

"No, I swear I'm not. They were in my family, and I saved them for now. No one is after me, no one will come looking. I have some beautiful tools."

She heard her father walking back and forth in front of the door, pacing as he did when he had a decision to make. She wanted the man to stay. She had never met anyone outside her own family.

"You'll work for me in the fields. I'll take what I want from what you've got. You'll stay away from the women. I'll watch you every minute. And if a priest's men come looking for you, I'll kill you myself."

"Fair," the young man said.

"Your horse can graze there, and you stay in the shed with him at night. You can have a meal now, then we'll deal."

Donna stepped away from the window just as the two men entered the house.

"This is Bennett," her father said. "He'll be staying a

day or two, in the shed. We'll have some bread and cheese now." The two men sat at the rough board table, and Donna and her mother set bread, milk, and cheese before them. She saw that Bennett was very hungry. She wanted to watch him eat, but her father pointed at the door of the little room, cut in half by a heavy curtain, that she shared with her brothers, and told her not to come out until the front door closed behind them. She sat down on her bed and picked up some sewing. As she worked, she thought about Bennett. He was taller than her father, but not as strong-looking. The quick smile he had given her when he'd entered the house was, she thought, a very pleasant sight.

He ate with the family every night, but Donna never spoke to him and hardly looked at him. She knew her father wouldn't like it and might even send him away. But sometimes they would look directly at each other, then quickly away again. The evening of the fourth day of his visit, her father sent everyone to their beds after the meal, and he and Bennett stayed up late, sitting at the table and talking in low voices. Donna could not try to overhear their conversation; her part of the room was farthest from the door.

The next morning at breakfast, her father was silent and ate very little. Bennett had taken his breakfast to the fields, as always. Donna was frightened. She had never seen her father behave this way. He looked ill, and her mother looked as if she might cry. Finally, he pushed away his bowl and stood up.

"I have something to say." He looked directly at Donna. "Bennett is leaving today, and Donna, you're going with him. You're old enough now. You'll be his woman. He'll make a good life for you." Joe, the youngest, began to cry. The two older boys stopped eating to stare at Donna. "Get your things together now. He's waiting for you." He walked slowly to where his daughter sat, held her for a moment, and, indicating with a wave of his arm that the boys were to precede him, walked out the door. Donna's mother got up from the table and left the room, returning with something shiny in her cupped hands. She opened them to show Donna a silver bracelet and a gold ring set with a purple stone.

"We'll be able to get that new bull now," she said, her face wet with tears. "I'll just put them away and help you pack."

Bennett was working in the bean field, hoeing, breaking the hard surface of the soil around the stalks. I sat on the hillside tending the goats, looking down at the village, watching the man, solitary among the rows of young vines still unstaked.

The sun was warm for early spring. I nearly dozed, daydreaming, thinking of Sunny and of the last time we made love, two nights before. It had been oddly calm. I had reached for her, and she had turned to me, slowly. We held each other, the length of our bodies close, her breasts soft against mine. The embrace seemed to last a long time. She pressed closer, held tighter. Our bodies began to move, rocking. There was no urgency, only great tenderness. We held each other, moving together, waiting for the feeling to change, waiting for the warmth to change to heat. She stroked my back, I stroked hers. We kissed, softly at first. I felt her tongue probe, tentative, between my lips, and pressed it with mine. I began to feel the first flickers of passion, but in a subdued way, subdued by her silence and my own. My hand had been resting on her hip. I began to knead with my fingers, feeling the softness, the firmness, the smoothness of her skin. Feeling her breasts against me, I wanted to touch them and moved back slightly to reach between us and cup her nipple in my palm. She sighed. I moved my hand back over her shoulder, to her nape, caressing the warm place where the hair started from the delicate skin. We kissed again, longer, and her mouth softened against mine. The thought of kissing became lost in the connection of our bodies.

I remembered wondering, after our lovemaking, when I had become so conscious of softening my mouth. I remembered that my breath had quickened, that I wanted to touch and be touched, but the calm awareness of all our movements had remained, and my thoughts had kept wandering to the most mundane details of my daily life. It hadn't been that way a while ago. I had only vague, emotional memories of those other times. I had been too caught up then to be aware of what we did or how we did it. There had been cycles in our four years together, alternating closeness and distance, but we had always come back again to lovemaking that was tender but urgent, loving, sensual, and deep, so deep that it was barely conscious, nearly mindless. Always before, anyway. I hadn't felt that way for a long time. Weeks, maybe even months. We had not achieved that depth this time, either. We had made love, but it had missed. We had missed really feeling each other.

I began to feel sad and pulled my mind away from that night and back to the reality of the day I was living. I looked down the hill again, to the field where Bennett was working. He was no longer alone. Freedom was with him, talking and smiling. He was smiling, too, leaning on his hoe. He looked relaxed. She stood tense, stolid, her arms crossed at her chest. I wondered what they were talking about. Some work or other, I imagined, although she did seem to be smiling a great deal. She glanced up at me and waved. A few minutes later she left him to his work. He watched her go, then returned to his hoeing.

With only Bennett's monotonous labor to watch, I retreated into my own mind again, searching for pleasant thoughts, circling around in my own head until I settled on the night before.

The evening had begun with a restless search for diversion, the kind of restless search that rarely turns up anything good. Sunny and I had gone for a walk, not sure of our destination. As we passed Diana's house, my mother and Angel came out the door. They were going, they said, to the Little Flower, a cafe Freedom had opened the year before. It had become a gathering place, a center for talk and entertainment. We decided to go with them.

The cafe was not far from the house where Diana and Angel lived. It was a small, one-room structure built of weathered wood. Freedom had put in a dozen round wooden tables, each with a crock of bright flowers at its center. A large stone fireplace stretched across half a wall.

Three of the tables were occupied. At one, Angel's daughter, Firstborn, was talking loudly to Redwood and Freedom about her most recent agricultural experiment, while Firstborn's daughter, Athena, sat some distance away near the fireplace with Calliope and Ocean. Luna held the third table with one companion, Sara. They were so engrossed in their conversation they barely noticed us come in. I was surprised to see the two of them together, considering Luna's attitude toward founders. I was also surprised to see Sara listening so intently to what I knew must be another of Luna's orations.

I wasn't interested in Firstborn's attempts to torture perfectly good grain into more suitable mutations, nor did I want to hear about Luna's preoccupation, the new settlement. Her movement had gained popularity since Bennett's arrival. He and Donna were living representatives of what had been, to the daughters at least, a mythical world. And Luna was using that revelation; we weren't safe in our village, or so went her latest argument. We could not protect ourselves without more knowledge and without expanding our power. Possibly she was right, but I knew only that the more successful she was, the more I disliked her.

Diana, Angel, and Sunny sat down with Luna and Sara. I joined my friends near the fireplace just as Ocean was saying, "Yes, but if Donna has a girl, there's no problem."

"No problem? With Bennett?" Calliope set down her tea cup definitively. "I wish I had your capacity for optimism, sweetheart. Hi, Morgan." I smiled at her and sat down. "Same old subject, endless possibilities."

"Well," Athena said, "what if she does have a boy?"

"Isn't there an old saying," I said wearily, "about crossing bridges when you come to them?" I was upset because Sunny had gone to sit with the others. Athena thought my irritation was aimed at her and looked insulted until I took her hand and muttered, "Sorry."

We tried to talk about other things, work we were doing, classes we were teaching, motherhood, but every topic brought up a point about Donna or Bennett. Athena, who worked with Angel in health care, confided that Donna had refused to be examined and was ignoring their pregnancy advice. One of Calliope's young students had told her that Bennett had been asking where our babies came from. Ocean, who had been helping Donna learn the work of the village, said the frail stranger could sew and cook, but hadn't the stamina for working in the fields.

I didn't realize how often I'd been looking at Sunny's table, where she sat next to Luna, listening and talking with apparent interest, until Athena caught me at it. She touched my arm.

"Everything all right?" I nodded. She smiled at me. I

was relieved, half an hour later, when Sunny joined us. She was cheerful and affectionate with me. The Flower was getting more crowded, conversations less serious, and my friends had been relieved of the obligation to treat me delicately.

Now, on my hillside, looking down at the man working below me, I felt sated, tired of digesting thoughts and feelings. I wanted to do something. My opportunity for activity was right down there, in the bean field. He was working hard, sweat running between the coils of muscle in his back. He'd been with us for two weeks, but I hadn't quite gotten used to seeing him: the strange coarseness of his skin, particularly the skin of his face; the way the muscles bunched in his shoulders. I had muscles too, of course, but his were thicker, more obvious. I wondered if he might be stronger than I. I had grown up on stories of the brutality of men, the way many of the strong ones used their strength. But I had also been taught that my own well-trained body was a match for his or any other man's, should it ever need to be, and that my speed, grace, and skill could make nothing of extra muscle weight.

I left the goats grazing on the hill and strolled down to the field.

"Hey, Bennett."

"Morgan." His reply was nearly a grunt, tilted upward in question at the end. He didn't stop hoeing.

"You're working hard."

He turned his angry face to me and stood straight, holding the hoe at his side like a spear. "Yes, I'm working hard. I earn my keep, even if I am a prisoner."

I couldn't deny that he was a prisoner. I'd thought a great deal about his enforced stay in our village and how it must feel to be watched constantly; the woman leaning casually against the tree, fifty feet from the edge of the bean field, was his guard for the day. I believed, as the founders did, that we had no choice: our security and our future depended on estrangement from the outside world. Not knowing what to say, I squatted beside a vine and stroked a rough, dry bottom leaf. He stood staring at me, forcing me to look up at him. I did, directly into his angry eyes.

"You're all scared of me," he said sullenly. "Every time I ask some little question you just look at me and shut up. Women and their secrets."

"Isn't it comfortable here? Don't you have everything you need to live?"

He thrust the hoe handle into the broken soil. It stood upright, quivering. "No!" he shouted, "I do not have everything I need to live." I stood to face him. "This is not my place. This is your village, your land. A woman's village." He looked disgusted. I remained silent, waiting for him to say more. "Leave me alone," he said. "Let me work. That's all there is for me to do here." He glared at me. "Why don't you say something?"

"You're here now. You're going to be staying. What can I say?"

"This is wrong," he said, his voice low and harsh. He pulled the hoe from the ground and held it in his two hands like a stick of kindling to be broken. "It's unnatural. It's against all law. I want to be in my own world. I'm a man. I can't live here." He paused, looking at his hands on the hoe, and spoke softly, "I can't breathe."

"I'm sorry. Your world is a man's world, isn't it? How do the women live then?"

"With their men, as they were meant to do." He looked pleased with himself, like a sly child. "And if you want to know anything else, that's too bad. It's a secret." He began to break the soil again. I decided not to be dismissed.

"Are you very strong, Bennett?" He straightened again and looked at me, his face hard.

"As men go, I'm strong enough." He smiled strangely, "Want me to show you?"

I was wary, remembering what I'd heard about men, but I knew I couldn't really be injured with my village within shouting distance.

"How would you do that? Show me, I mean?" He laughed, threw down the hoe, and lunged at me. I was not caught off guard, seeing the look in his eyes. I spun away to the side, narrowly avoiding an irrigation ditch still muddy with spring rain. He stumbled, caught himself, and twisted around, reaching for me with both hands.

"Why aren't you screaming for your friends?" he jeered, glancing at the guard under the tree. She was watching, but I knew she would not interfere. And I would not allow myself to be distracted by conversation. I ignored his question and waited, ready for his next lunge. He feinted once, twice, danced back laughing, feinted again, and surprised me. I felt the weight of his body pressing me to the ground. I twisted my leg out from under and kicked for his side, catching him hard beneath the ribs. He grunted, rolled away, recovered, and was on me again before I could move. He straddled my thigh, and I could feel the place between his legs growing hard.

"See? That's how strong I am. Stronger than any damned woman." I was afraid, repelled by the smell and feel of his body, but I would not shout for help. "You just remember this. When you hear some woman giving me orders. When you think you've got me caught. You remember this." He got up suddenly, turned his back to me, picked up the hoe, and began to work. He was strong, yes, and quick. But I knew I had not done my best.

"You're a good fighter, Bennett. And you've beaten me once. But I don't think you can beat me twice." I said it quietly, conversationally, as I would speak to another woman. I was not prepared for the reaction I caused. His face turned red with anger.

"Get out of my sight, you whore!" he screamed at me.

"Do I have to teach you again?" I had not been angry, and I didn't understand his anger.

"There's no need to get upset. I was just wondering if you were planning to be in the games and we could try again, that's all."

"Games?" His face had returned to its normal color. He looked interested.

"Contests. About two weeks from now. We have them every month."

"Fighting?"

"Well, yes, and sports. I think you should be in them. I think you'd be very good."

His anger had faded completely. His expression was now one of amused contempt. "Fight against a bunch of women? What do I get for winning?"

"It's usually a work holiday, or extra supplies of something, or a favored job. Whatever the judges decide."

"Maybe I'll do it, just for fun. Now leave me alone." I didn't like the tone with which he said it, but anyone, after all, has the right to be left alone. I went back to my goats, back to the hillside, back to watching him work in the field. He was so strange. I didn't understand his reasons for anger. They didn't seem to be anything like mine. He acted as though he were constantly being gravely insulted.

IV

It was a chilly evening, just turned dark. I was working on some papers my composition class had handed in that day. Sunny was pacing the living room. From time to time, she would stand at the window gazing out, or sit crossing and uncrossing her legs, or read over my shoulder as I worked. I thought she might be settling down when she took a book from the shelf, one of the books the founders had brought with them. The author was a woman who had written several books during the early seventies. I loved her writing, although there were references and modes of thought that were too alien for me to comprehend. I found her world terrifying, painfully complex, and brutal in an archaic way. My mother had helped me with my first reading. Although the book was written before she was born, it described a world she could understand.

Sunny pawed through it, stopped and read briefly, flipped through a few pages, stopped and read again, and then put it down on the table beside me.

"Absolutely impossible. What are all those funny little marks in it?"

I glanced irritably at the page she was pointing to. "Those are the places I marked to ask my mother about. It's a great book," I added defensively.

"Goat droppings. It doesn't make any sense."

"Neither did her world."

"It's gone now, anyway. It's been gone for fifty years. It's irrelevant." She paused. "I keep wondering what it's like out there now."

I knew that Luna was having a new settlement meeting the next night and suspected that Sunny's "wondering" was a prelude to a discussion about that. Why, I thought angrily, was she being so oblique? I felt my stomach tighten and forced myself to breathe deeply, to relax, to keep away the nausea that made it so hard for me to cope with emotional scenes. I was afraid of challenging her dishonesty. I'd been afraid for weeks, watching her spend more time away from me, time with Luna and her friends. She alternated between treating me gently, almost politely, and erupting in quick irritation for no reason I could see.

I pretended to return to my papers, saying as lightly as I could and with as much finality as I could manage, "Not much different from what it was like before, I suppose."

"Before?" she said indignantly. "You mean forty years ago? That's ridiculous. Even the little that Donna could tell us proves things have changed."

She wasn't going to stop. I would have to continue arguing as though I were defending myself. So I brought us to the point. "It's the new settlement, isn't it? That's what you're really talking about." I felt as though I'd lifted up a rotting log. I had a good idea of what I'd find, but I didn't really want to look at it.

"Well, it's time for one. We can't grow much more here. What if this woman—" she waved the book at me,

"—started a village?" I began to answer, saying that there was no way we could ever know, that the woman was long dead anyway, but she turned her head, brushing away my words. "What if thousands of women started villages? What if we could find each other? And what about Bennett?"

"What about Bennett?" I asked her. I didn't want to go anywhere. I didn't feel safe enough with Sunny any more to go off with her, away from my home and friends. But I didn't want her to go anywhere, either.

"He's here, that's what about him. We've been sitting here tucked away all these years, and they walk right in on us. You think we're safe with a lot of Bennetts running around in the world? Maybe some of Luna's ideas are a little extravagant, but she's right about one thing. If we don't have a thousand villages, we'd better start thinking about having them."

"We don't know if we can even survive a hundred miles from here," I said, shaking my head. "And what does this all have to do with us, anyway, with you and me?"

"We ought to know," she said, ignoring my question. "We really ought to know." She said the last word vehemently, almost angrily. I was silent. I agreed with her. But I didn't want to be one of those who found out first hand.

"Luna's having a meeting tomorrow night." There it was. She'd finally gotten to it.

"Yes, I know."

"I'm going. Do you want to come with me?"

It was more a challenge than a question. Angry and almost in tears, I agreed to go. I was interested in the meeting, in finding out how real the new settlement was. I had expected that we would go. But I'd had an absurd, half-conscious little fantasy, I realized now, about how we would talk about going, and my fantasy conversation was nothing like the one we'd just had. She announced that she was going out for a while, got a sweater from the bedroom, and said good night politely. After she'd closed the door behind her, I put my papers aside and allowed myself the bitter amusement of playing out the fantasy in my mind. She would have said, "Let's not go to the meeting. Let's have a quiet evening at home together. We can hear about it afterward." And I would have said, "Oh, we should go for a while, just to see what's going on. We can leave when we get bored."

The next morning I went looking for Sara. I'd seen her talking to Luna several times, and Luna rarely talked about anything but her "movement." Sara would know what was going on. Of course I couldn't ask her directly about Sunny, but maybe I would learn something, prepare myself somehow for the meeting that night.

I found her supervising a gang of helpers and apprentices who were putting up a new house. She was pointing at a long, heavy piece of wood propped up on sawhorses and talking to an embarrassed-looking youngster. I stood back and waited, trying not to hear, but the young woman saw me and looked even more uncomfortable.

"This beam's too long by a good inch," Sara barked. "Now cut it right." The helper began to measure the beam. "And don't cut it too short, either," Sara snapped, turning and noticing me.

"Oh!" she said, a bit embarrassed herself. "No one was supposed to catch me being the obnoxious boss." I laughed. Sara was not known for her gentle treatment of young carpenters. "Did you want to talk to me?" I nodded. "Come on, then." She led me away from the building site, sat down under a tree, and patted the ground beside her, inviting me to sit. She yawned, stretched her wiry body, and looked at me from under her heavy black brows. I didn't know how to open the conversation, so she gave me more time.

"Look at that, Morgan," she said, waving at the raw framework, the sturdy-looking crew. "Another new house.

Twenty more years we'll fill the valley."

Startled, I stared at her. I'd never really thought about our growing population. "Really? Twenty years?"

She shrugged and smiled. "I'm exaggerating a little. Thirty or forty?"

"Is that why you're so interested in the new settlement?"

She scowled and placed her strong brown hand on my arm. "I don't know, Morgan. It makes a lot of sense. The hardest work seems to be done here." She glanced again at the women building the house. "They can do it—construction, repair, anything."

"They still need your supervision," I objected.

"No." She shook her head. "There are three, maybe four, daughters who could take over all my work right now." She smiled, looking at my sad face. "It's all right. I'm not depressed about it. That's what I trained them for."

I had been thinking of Sunny. "How does Joanna feel about all this?"

She stood up. "Come have lunch with us. Ask her yourself." She cupped her hands around her mouth and yelled "Lunch!" and the carpenters began sawing the last few strokes, pounding the last nail, putting away their tools. Sara put an arm around my shoulder, and we walked together toward the dining hall. "We've been talking about it for a while now. She's got some objections. We've had some fights." She chuckled. "Last night I accused her of getting old. She told me to set up housekeeping with an eighteen-year-old." I laughed. At least they were talking. "She thinks it's too dangerous, and of course she's right. Dangerous for the ones who go. Dangerous for the ones who stay. She didn't have to remind me that we barely got here with our lives forty years ago. But maybe people aren't as hungry and desperate as they were then." She paused, thoughtful. "She remembers the other world, too. The one we grew up in. We rejected it, and we left it behind, but it's still part of us. And I want to find out what happened to it."

We passed a washhouse. Freedom, coming out the door with a basket of laundry, waved to us. "I was hoping we could get some information out of Bennett," Sara said, "but he won't even tell her anything much," she indicated Freedom, "and she's nice to him!" I laughed. "Got to get to that washhouse when the rains stop. Roof leaked all winter." We walked on past the dome where Sara lived with Joanna. "I wonder whatever possessed me to think I'd like living in a round house." She shook her head. We skirted a small field I had helped to plow the autumn before for this year's tomatoes and cut down the path that led to the main road and the dining hall. Children were playing in the school yard. "They'll be having classes in the yard if we don't get to that addition soon." Sara saw everything through the eyes of a builder; she was involved in the life of the village in a basic everyday way. I wondered if my function as historian didn't remove me from her kind of reality.

Joanna was waiting at a small table near the door. It was still early and the dining hall was nearly empty, but the women working kitchen duty that day were already standing behind the long counter, chatting among themselves, waiting to ladle out large servings of vegetable stew to the hungry women who would be coming in over the next three hours. Sara waved me to a chair beside Joanna and went to the counter to get lunch for all of us, carrying it back on a big wooden tray. She sat down and began to toy with her food.

Although Sara's invitation to me had been casual enough, I felt tension between them and began to feel shy about bringing up the subject of the new settlement. It occurred to me with horror that Sara might have invited me to serve as a buffer. Sara was too quiet. I felt Joanna looking at me.

"Don't be uncomfortable, Morgan," she said. "Obviously we've been fighting, but you know us well enough to know that doesn't mean very much. Sara's not really sulking; she's just waiting for us to talk to each other and take her off the hook."

"What hook?" Sara demanded indignantly.

Joanna didn't quite laugh. "So innocent."

"Don't be smug," Sara said more quietly.

Joanna lifted her hands, palms up in surrender. "Okay, talk about it. You too, Morgan. Did she bring you as an ally?"

"No!" I said a little too loudly. Joanna looked pleased. I felt as though I'd been put in the middle of an argument between my mother and Angel. These two were close family to me. Sometimes even now, after so many years of adulthood, I found it difficult to think of myself as grown up in their presence. Friction between them terrified me, as a child is terrified. I needed a moment to place myself more surely in the context of friend. Joanna, sensitive to my misery, turned all her attention toward Sara and spoke to her pleasantly.

"How's the job going?"

"Same old stuff."

I ate doggedly, looking aimlessly around the dining hall. Bennett and Donna had come in. He was demanding a double helping of food, even though there was no limit to the number of times one could return to the counter for more.

I saw Joanna glance at him with distaste. She was talking softly to Sara. "Well, maybe you just need to do something different for a while."

"I don't think that would help."

"How about a vacation, then? We could hop down to Disneyland . . ."

Sara laughed. I returned my full attention to my two friends.

"Very funny," Sara said. "Don't you ever get tired of sticking stones together?"

"Hey, I like building fireplaces. It's making shoes, milking goats, shearing sheep, plowing fields, and picking apples—that's what gets boring. Same old thing, day after day." She drew me back into the conversation. "What do you think about all this new settlement stuff, Morgan?"

I laughed. I had come to lunch to ask her that question. "I think it's causing a lot of trouble. And we don't need any more than what we have already." I glared meaningfully in Bennett's direction.

"But that's the whole point," Sara said impatiently. She looked intensely at Joanna. "You remember what it was like—when we left."

"Sure. Chaos. Killing. Everything going to hell. No law. No order. No power. No food. Starving people running all over the place stealing from other starving people. The end of the world. Plague. Religious fanatics. Land and water and people and animals poisoned by nuclear leaks. Everything shut down. Cities torn to pieces. Who wants to think about all that? That's what we ran away from." She was angry with the pain of remembering. I'd heard that anger before from other elders, but never from Joanna, who always said she preferred living in the present.

"Right. Chaos. And nothing stays that way. They've created some kind of order. And we know a little about it." She nodded toward the woman and man across the room.

"Yeah. All the more reason to avoid it. Priests, yet. Wouldn't they just love to burn us at the stake?"

Sara turned to me. "Morgan, reason with her."

"I don't—" I stuttered.

"Okay. I'll try again. The point is, we can't avoid it. It came here. It isn't going to leave us alone. It's not the new settlement so much that I'm talking about, although that's going to happen sooner or later. I'm talking about going out and having a look. I think we'd better start thinking about defending ourselves. And I don't mean sitting here hiding and pretending we're the only people in the world." She speared the last piece of potato on her plate and swallowed it without chewing.

Joanna raised her hands and slapped both of them palm down, hard, on the table. "Well, fine. That's just fine. You go ahead and have a look, while I sit here and have a nervous breakdown. Then, if you make it back alive, we can talk about this new settlement some more."

The dining hall was getting crowded. It was time for us to leave to make room for the later arrivals. I stood up, but Sara grabbed my arm, holding me there. She spoke to both of us. "We'd have two villages, not just one. We'd be stronger. We could trade with each other . . ."

"I see the point," Joanna said, rising. "I understand. I just don't have the nerve to go out there first. I want someone else to do it." Her dark blue eyes looked hard and sad all at once. "I wish it didn't have to be you."

We parted at the door. I kissed them both, and as we were saying goodbye, Bennett and Donna brushed past us, their guard trailing behind. I watched him walk away and felt a shudder of disgust and anger. He was to blame, I told myself. This was all his fault.

V

"Going to the meeting tonight, Morgan?" Athena and I were working a full day in the fields, plowing under the debris of winter vegetables in a section of land that Firstborn had marked for soybeans in her complex system of crop rotation.

I was enjoying the work. Physical labor rested my mind. After a day of plowing or harvesting I never knew what I'd been thinking about, or if indeed I'd done any thinking at all. Athena's question was an intrusion on my happy mindlessness. Suddenly I felt tired.

"Let's take a break, okay?" She agreed and we walked to the edge of the field. I lay down full length on the grass, stretching, and she sat beside me. "We're going," I admitted finally. "Are you?"

"I guess so. Are you going to get more involved in it?"

"How do you mean?" I said noncommittally.

"Are you going to go away?"

"No one's going anywhere yet." Why was she hounding me? Hadn't I made it clear by my attitude that I didn't have anything to say?

"Of course. That's true." I examined her averted face, speculating on possible reasons for her questions. Was there gossip about Sunny and me? Probably, but unlike her mother, Firstborn, Athena didn't usually pry to confirm a rumor. Was she personally interested? Why? Suddenly horrified, I caught myself and forced my mind back under the control of my reason. What was wrong with me? I was letting my emotional problems make me crazy. Poor Athena was probably just making conversation, and I was looking for unpleasant motives where there were none. I had gotten too used to watching Sunny, trying to discover her moods, trying to read her thoughts.

"Let's get back to work," I said, putting my arm around Athena. Her skin was warm through her thin shirt. I felt companionable and affectionate and guilty for my temporary madness. When we parted in the late afternoon I called lightly after her, "See you at the meeting!"

It was early evening when Sunny and I set out, walking silently toward the meeting house. In contrast to my anxiety and Sunny's tension, the village was peaceful in the pale light of a quarter-moon. I tried to concentrate, Sara-fashion, on the physical life around me. Although the spring nights were still cold, women sat outside their houses talking and nodding to passersby. When I saw Angel and Redwood on Redwood's front step, I stopped for a moment to say hello. Redwood had a cat on her lap, and the two older women were laughing and petting the animal.

"Another pregnant one," Angel told me, taking the cat up in her round, soft arms. Sunny, who had stopped a few paces beyond the house, walked slowly back to us.

"Time to start creating some disinterested toms," Redwood said. Angel grimaced. She disliked performing even minor surgery, but animal birth control was her responsibility. This cat, like all the cats and dogs in the village, was a descendant of the starved and hunted animals that had found a home in the valley. They earned their keep with more than companionship and charm. The cats provided rodent control at the grain bins; the dogs helped with the sheep and were trained to pull small loads in carts. I stroked the tabby where the life inside her had stretched her belly taut.

"Too bad we don't have an herb that'll do it," I said.

"A Demeter flower in reverse?" Angel laughed.

Sunny touched my arm. "We should be going, Morgan." I nodded, said goodbye to the two elders, and we walked on. When we passed the woods we could hear the children laughing and shouting in the darkness, passing the remaining hour or so until bedtime in a game of hide and seek. The village was so safe, so familiar. And I loved it so much.

The meeting was not large. Perhaps three dozen women had gathered by the time we arrived. The building, which the original inhabitants of the valley had used as a church, had one large room with high ceilings and tall windows and a small office at the back which we never used. The benches held nearly a hundred people comfortably. Women were clustered in small groups, some in the front rows closest to the council table and dais where the altar had once been, some far at the back, their attitude that of spectators. Luna was seated at the council table, the smiling center of an intense group. Just like her, I thought sourly, to take over the meeting hall for such a small gathering. She could just as well have had it at the Flower or her own house. No, it had to be on official territory, and she had to take the seat of authority.

Sunny left me just inside the door, saying "See you in a bit, okay?" and began moving through the room, greeting people, talking earnestly. I forced myself not to watch her and sat down in a back row next to Calliope and Ocean, my

41

refuge in the crowd. I was surprised to see them there and said so.

"Curiosity," Calliope said. Neither of them asked about my reasons for being there.

Luna had stepped down from her altar and was greeting newcomers. She paused at the end of our row and smiled broadly at us.

"Good to see you here." Her tone was hearty.

"Not a very big crowd, is it?" I said.

Her smile disappeared. "This is our first real meeting." She marched away, clapping her hands to attract attention, signaling the start of business. She made her way around the council table to the dais and opened the meeting.

"We're going to get right down to business by reading a list of committees some of the organizers feel will be needed to get things ready for the move." There was a surprised murmur in our part of the room. She was making it clear that the new settlement was a fact, not a proposal. She read from the list: weapons, tools, food, livestock, transport. "And of course we'll need scouts to go out in advance of the main party to find a site for the village. They'll leave as soon as we can get them ready to go."

I noticed Redwood, sitting in the row just ahead of us, nodding. I wondered if she was planning to go. Perhaps she was just interested in seeing how it would all be done this time. She had been the scout for Demeter, traveling north and east from the San Francisco Bay Area to find a warm and fertile valley in the Sierra foothills.

Luna asked if there were any questions.

"I've got one," Calliope called out. Luna looked irritated. "Why are you doing it? What's the point?"

Several of the women sitting closest to Luna shook their heads, but Luna answered seriously. "Three reasons. To expand our strength, to decentralize, and to have a look at what's out there."

"We know what's out there," I said. Luna glanced at me patronizingly and looked around the room for other questions.

Joanna spoke up from her seat near the front, next to Sara. "Donna and Bennett have given me some idea of what's out there. Sounds like trouble to me."

I was encouraged by the few little snickers her remark elicited. "How can you take the responsibility for the danger you'd expose the village to? You could be caught or followed. You could get those people out there—" I waved my arm vaguely "—interested enough to search these hills until they found us."

"We've already been found, Morgan." Sunny, sitting only a few feet from the dais, rose and turned to look at me. "It's true, as you say, that we have some idea of what's out there. The vacuum is filling. With Bennetts. Not with us. They're building villages. They've been doing it all along, while we've been waiting for them to come and find us." She sat, and I could feel everyone looking at me. The lines were forming. And now no one could avoid knowing that Sunny and I were on opposite sides of the issue. Even worse, we were on opposite sides of the room. In my misery, I hadn't noticed that Athena had slipped in to sit beside me. She stood, facing Luna.

"You're right about one thing, Luna. We do need to be stronger. But what you're talking about is scattering our strength. You want to take weapons and tools and seed and supplies with you, to divide our resources now, of all times. Why now?"

"Right!" Calliope jumped to her feet. "You're doing it now because it's easier to do it now. You can use Bennett to convince people to follow you, something to scare us with. I look at it another way. I say he's brought us problems to face right here, problems we can't run away from."

Luna was angry now and she let it show. "Not running from. Advancing on. We have to go, and if there are other

43

villages like this, we have to find them." During the scattering of applause that followed Luna's words I looked toward Sunny, trying to see how she was reacting. I couldn't see her, and I thought it was just as well. Maybe if I could stop seeing the new settlement through the fabric of our relationship I would know how I really felt about it. Even though I was fighting the idea, I wanted to be objective and to decide for myself and with nothing clouding my judgment whether it was a reasonable, courageous plan or a way to stir things up, create excitement, grab some power and attention.

"Find them?" Calliope was saying. "Who are we going to find? You'll be lucky if you can find your way back here without getting us all killed." Although she spoke well, and I saw fear on several faces, Calliope could not break through the mood that Luna was creating. In the silence that followed my friend's words, Luna asked for volunteers for the committees she had named. Sara stood, her hand on Joanna's shoulder, and volunteered to be a scout. She was cheered.

Someone called out, "How about you, Redwood? You've got experience!"

"Hell, no!" Redwood roared. "I'm not ready to go back out there."

I saw a hand go up in the front row, Sunny's hand, her yellow shirtsleeve falling back against her upper arm.

"I'll go," she said. My stomach turned over. I felt dizzy and hot. I don't know how long I sat there, too stunned to move. It was probably only a few seconds before I stood and pushed my way blindly past Athena and across the acre of floor space to the door, knowing my flight was creating a reaction in the room, but unable to stay and pretend that I had known what Sunny was planning. I stopped just outside and tried to catch my breath.

"Morgan?" It was Sunny's voice. She had come out the door after me. I didn't look up.

"What are you doing out here?" I demanded. "Your meeting isn't over yet."

"Morgan, we need to talk."

"Talk?" I said softly. I wanted to scream, but we were still close to the meeting hall. "I think we needed to talk before now." I began to walk away from the building, out onto the road. She wanted to talk? We'd talk, but not here. We'd talk where I felt free to scream. Or do anything else I felt like doing. I walked toward our own house, where I could close the door and break the furniture. She followed a pace behind me.

The worst of it was the contrast with Sara and Joanna. They were together, even though they didn't agree. Sara had talked to Joanna. They had sat together at the meeting.

Sunny had caught up with me and was walking beside me. "Maybe I should have talked to you, told you what I was planning." I said nothing. "I just haven't known what to say. I'm not sure I know yet." She was silent for the length of a deep breath. I could feel myself shifting from rage to fear and back again. I didn't break the silence. "This is a beautiful and peaceful place, isn't it?" She gestured around us at the village, echoing thoughts I'd had earlier in the evening. "But there's nothing to struggle against. When we were growing up, things were still difficult and uncertain. But now it's all easy. Everything is repetition. Everything is like the games—something to pass the time and keep us from getting soft." Her mood was changing from nervous uncertainty to a purposefulness I'd never really seen in her before. We passed the woods. They were silent, the children all gone home to bed. "When Bennett came—he comes from out there, and it's so big and there's so much. Don't you ever feel as though you need to see it?"

I turned on her. "Joanna knew what Sara was planning to do. They talked."

We had come to the door of our house, but Sunny held back, reluctant, it seemed, to go in. "I agree with Luna," she said stubbornly, ignoring the issue I was raising, sticking tightly to the one that was settled. "We have to go."

"Why? Why are you so intent on dying out there?"

"I'm intent on living. On seeing for myself."

"But you've heard our mothers talk. You've heard Bennett talk. You've heard Donna—she doesn't talk." My words sounded confused, panicky, and I realized it.

"Our mothers, yes. Their coming here was positive. It was an experiment, a brave thing to do. The right thing to do. I would have done the same thing. Sometimes," she added harshly, "I think you would have stayed out there, rather than change your life."

I gasped, astounded at her judgment of me. "You're calling me a coward. You!" I shouted at her. Two women passing by turned to stare at us. I opened the door and pushed Sunny inside. She was too startled to stand her ground. I slammed the door behind us. "You were so afraid to confront me with your plans that you waited for a meeting to do it. You sat on the other side of the room, with thirty people between us, and told me you were leaving. You're the coward."

"And I suppose you didn't know what was going on? I didn't notice you confronting me. Creeping around, watching me . . ."

"You shit!" I screamed at her, crying. I tried to hit her, but she caught my fist in both her hands, and I suddenly felt too weak to follow through.

"All right," she said. "Let's talk. Let's talk about why things have happened the way they have. We'll build a fire and drink wine and talk this out." Her voice trembled slightly, but I thought she was much calmer than I was. She was ready to talk now, and I didn't want to. I didn't want to hear what she might have to say. I nodded and went to the fireplace, taking dry leaves and twigs from the kindling box, slowly, breaking some larger kindling, laying it all on the grate. I was trying to stop crying. I rubbed the back of my hand across my eyes before I noticed the black smudge of soot across my knuckles. Sunny was pouring the wine. I fetched three logs from the pile outside the front door. She set the wine goblets on the table near the fireplace. I piled the logs on top of the kindling, methodically, carefully, so the structure would not collapse. But finally I had to light the fire. I had to go to the table and sit across from her. I sipped my wine, knowing my eyes were red, not wanting to look up at her. She reached across the table and wiped the soot from my cheek. We waited for each other to speak. She spoke first.

"I was cowardly, I know. I think in a way I'm afraid of you, afraid of your disapproval. You're so mental. So logical. I knew you'd try to talk me out of it, talk me into confusion, attack me." She shrugged. "I couldn't face it."

"I'm to blame?" I asked incredulously. "Because you wanted to do something you didn't think I'd like? Because you just went ahead and did it without a word to me? Because you didn't care enough about me to try to work it out *with* me? You want to leave me. Why don't you just admit it?" Was I actually whining? To my ears, it sounded like I was. But I couldn't seem to help myself.

"No. It's not that I don't want to be with you, or that I want to be with someone else—"

"Not even Luna?" I jabbed nastily. I didn't like myself much for that one, but I was a little past caring.

Sunny shook her head. "Oh, Morgan, there's nothing . . . look, I just feel restless. I don't know why, for sure, but I do. I don't think I have any choice but to do this on my own for my own reasons."

"You don't think! You don't know!" I wanted to hit her again and realized that my fists were pressed tight against the table. She reached over to touch my arm. I moved it away, and she withdrew her hand.

"Please," she said. She was crying now. "Please listen. This feeling I have now, it goes away sometimes when I'm loving you the most and working, and just living, but when it comes back again, I'm angry that I ever lost it. You're capable of contentment, of living happily where you are, of being here. I'm a builder, Morgan. I need to build something new."

"You really want to leave." I said it slowly. A statement, not a question.

"No, I don't want to leave. I wish I'd already gone and come back. But I haven't gone. Not anywhere. I can't stand not knowing, for myself. I'm afraid to go, but I have to."

Her words made me feel more hopeful. "Then you want to come back to stay?"

"I don't know." I wanted to scream at her, to make her say something definite.

"You've never even asked me if I wanted to be part of the new settlement. You treat it as something that has to separate us." I was complaining again. Why couldn't I stop?

"Well, isn't it?"

"I don't know," I said, like Sunny trying to believe that I truly didn't know. I rubbed my eyes and looked at her. "When are you going?"

"I have to talk to Sara about that, but I expect we'll be ready to go in a few days." She stood. "Look, I'm really exhausted. Why don't we go to bed, now, and if you want to talk about it more tomorrow, we can." She reached for me again, but I pushed her away. "Please, Morgan, sweetheart. Can't you see how important this is?" I shook my head. The tears were coming again. She sighed, stood beside me uncertainly for a moment, and went to bed.

I picked up the wine goblets to take to the kitchen. I was shaking and crying. I wasn't finished fighting yet. I wasn't ready for her to go to bed. I threw one of the goblets at the stone hearth—I think it was the one she'd been drinking from—and watched it shatter into bits of clay. I let the other one drop from my hand to the wooden floor. It rolled under the table. I sat there for a long time. The fire burnt away. I stared at it, thought of rebuilding it again, picked up a piece of kindling and splintered it in my hands. My left hand hurt. The skin was barely broken, a small sliver of wood embedded in my palm. I began to pace, feeling cold, talking to myself. It wasn't real. Our talk, her leaving—they weren't real. I began to cry again, still pacing, until, exhausted and sick, I lay down on the floor before the dead fire and sobbed until I was too cold, too tired, and then I went to bed. Sunny was asleep. Just before dawn, I fell asleep too.

She was already out of the house when I awoke at my usual time, got out of bed, and went to look at myself in the mirror. My face was puffy. The freckles stood out like spots of dye on my pale face. My eyes looked terrible. She would come back to be with me, I thought philosophically, or I would get over it and wouldn't love her any more. I laced my boots over a pair of woolen socks, the soft texture and the smell recalling the sheep shearing more than a year before, when we'd worked so well together. Sunny, with her sensitive nose, always hated shearing time. But I had made her laugh at the antics of the silly animals.

I pulled a sweater over my shirt, left the house, and went to breakfast. I was relieved to see that Sunny was not there.

Firstborn looked at me closely when I sat down near her. She kept glancing at me, hoping to start a conversation. I wanted only to eat and get to my morning's work. I ate quickly, wished a good day to the women at my table, and started off alone.

As I walked past the building where Calliope spent most of her working hours building and repairing parts for her generators, she came out the door and called to me. I really didn't want to talk, not even to her. She looked as though she were about to say something consoling. I forestalled her.

"I hear we may be running short on power," I said. "How are things going?"

"I'm not too worried. I wish we had a little more in storage than we do, to hold us until spring really gets going."

"It was a long gray winter."

"That's true," she said, continuing to go along with my diversion. "We may have to go to some hand-production by the end of the month."

"Hand-production," I said, with a good imitation of interested distaste. "I hate those old foot-treadle machines. I always feel like I've spent the day hopping."

She laughed generously. "Yeah. We need another windmill. That would have helped this year."

"Good idea. Well, I'll see you later, okay?"

"Sure. Where will you be today?"

"Shoe factory this morning, chronicle this afternoon."

"Are you being strong, or is it just that you can't talk about it yet?"

"I'm not that strong."

"They'll come back. They have to. I'm postponing my Demeter ceremony until they do."

"An act of faith," I said, trying to smile at her.

"If you need to get out of the house, you know you can stay with us for a few days. And when you're ready to talk, I'll be ready to listen."

I nodded, kissed her, and went to work.

Athena came to see me that afternoon at the chronicle. I was wary, not wanting her sympathy, but she didn't offer any. She had a project she wanted me to help her with.

"You know that old cowboy hat Angel's been dragging around for forty years?"

I smiled. "Her special occasion hat?"

"Right. Well, it finally collapsed into a heap of straw. Fell apart. She's devastated." Angel had brought the hat to Demeter with her and had kept it carefully packed away,

50

bringing it out only rarely, trying to keep it in one piece as long as possible. None of the hats we made in the village for field work seemed to suit her as well.

"That's too bad," I said, wondering what she was getting at.

"I want to make her another one just like it if I can, for her birthday. But I can't do it alone."

"I don't understand."

"I want it to be a surprise. And there's not enough left of the old one to get a size from, so I have to measure her head." I stared at her, confused. "I can't just measure her head, don't you see? She'd know."

"You want to measure my head?"

"I want to measure everyone's head. Tell people I'm doing a study."

"You don't think they'll think that's a little odd?"

"Sure, but they'll tolerate it. And she won't know what I'm doing."

I burst out laughing. "So you want me to help you measure heads?"

She smiled and nodded.

"Okay," I said. She kissed me on the cheek and went away again. At least, I thought, Athena's battered-heart remedy had worked for a few minutes. She had made me laugh.

VI

Three days on the road, and Sunny hadn't seen anything more exotic than a ruined old highway, its surface crazed, broken and lifted in chunks by weather and the encroaching grasses, buried in places by winter-sliding hillside. She had thought at the time that Morgan would have enjoyed seeing the road and knowing it went all the way to San Francisco. Morgan had been in her mind a great deal. Sunny was dissatisfied with the way they had parted, each trying to conceal her fear and sadness, Sunny trying and failing to conceal her eagerness to go. She missed her, and she felt guilty for hurting her. But at the same time she was perversely resentful toward Morgan for making her feel fettered by emotion when she was starting out on the greatest adventure of her life.

Adventure. So far, she had to admit, the novelties she had seen had barely outweighed the discomforts of travel.

She reached up under her shirt and tugged again at the

binding that wrapped her breasts. Sara, sitting beside her on the wagon seat, wagged her head sympathetically. "Hard to believe women used to tie themselves up that way all the time, isn't it?"

"I thought they used to make themselves stick out."

"Stuck out, squashed flat—what's the difference?"

"Yeah. But I guess it's worth it now."

"I'm sure it will be," Sara said grimly.

The two scouts were dressed in old and colorless pants, shirts, and loose jacket tunics. Their breasts were bound for concealment. They were assuming that the only safe way to travel in this world of Bennetts was disguised as men. Neither of them was sure she could pull off the difficult masquerade.

Their wagon carried grain, dried fruit, potatoes, and goods they hoped they could trade for fresh food along the way: baskets, pots, and woolen blankets. Everything they carried, including their weapons, had been selected after a series of consultations with the new settlement committees. They didn't expect to be traveling more than a month, even allowing for what Sunny called "adventure" and Sara called "learning the hard way." The plan was to travel southwest to the coast and back to Demeter along a route slightly to the south of their westward one. They were looking for information about centers of population and the ways people lived, but their primary goal was to find a secluded site for the new settlement.

They were traveling due south now, along the Sacramento River, looking for a place to cross. The landmarks would be familiar to Sara until they crossed, turned to the west, and headed into territory the founders had not covered on their way to the valley.

For hours after they had first sighted the river, Sara had avoided looking at it. She was remembering what it had been like before, on the way to Demeter, the bloated bodies caught along the banks and under a bridge far to the south of where they were now.

When Sunny requested a rest stop, Sara insisted they camp out of sight of the river.

Sunny settled in for her hour's rest with a map of Northern California. "There used to be a pretty good-sized town here to the south," she said, pointing at the yellowed sheet, stiff with new backing glued to it for their trip. "We ought to—"

"No, we oughtn't," Sara snapped, pacing, exercising her cramped legs. "There were no people left there forty years ago. Nothing but ruins. Besides, I don't want to go looking for trouble."

Sunny glared at her. "If there are no people, how could there be trouble?"

"It's on a main route. There might be people. And we're still too close to home to take chances."

Sunny wasn't satisfied, but she gave in. "Okay. I guess you're right this time. But I hope you're not going to be overcautious."

"Of course not. I just don't want to go leaping into . . . well, without looking . . ." She was having trouble with this argument. She was feeling more fear than was useful, remembering more than might be relevant. She frowned and lowered her eyes. "Joanna was right about one thing. I'm not liking it much, being out here. I'm afraid of towns. When you're living through something, it's not so bad. You can stand it because you have to. But you look back on it, and it gets worse. It grows. Don't worry though. I'll work on it."

Sunny softened. "Don't think I don't understand. I've heard about the things that happened."

"We kept your education pretty much to bare facts," Sara said wryly. "You had to be there."

"In the cities, you mean," Sunny prodded.

"Oh, anywhere," Sara said vaguely. She didn't want to talk about the cities.

* * *

"It's a terrible situation," Diana said mournfully.

"Hand me some nails, will you?" Sara replied.

"How can you be so casual about it?" Diana was outraged at her friend. She took the hammer from Sara's hand and a nail from the box on the floor. "Here, let me try that once. How can you just ignore two years of drought? There won't be enough food." She placed the nail carefully on the joint at the top of the cabinet Sara was building and hammered it in with a flourish. "There."

"You let the board move," Sara grumbled. "Now the top's crooked." She stuck a screwdriver in the joint and began to pry the pieces apart. The pressed board crumbled. "Damn! This stuff's no good." She sat back, disgusted, staring at the imperfect work.

"It won't show much, Sara."

The sixteen-year-old shook her head. "I wish I could get some real wood, just once."

"You ought to be worrying about getting real food," Diana said self-righteously. Sara shrugged. The drought would pass, no matter how much Diana insisted on worrying about it, and the next year there would be another reason for scarcity and inflation. The government was probably lying, anyway. Or maybe some of the new shortages would be permanent. So what. You couldn't go crazy every time something else important disappeared from the world. Her parents had told her about a time when people ate meat almost every day, when fuel and power were plentiful, when a person could find a space to be with silence around it. They had been her age when the realities of the eighties had cleared away the last soft-focus dream of the sixties, when the dreamers learned that you couldn't very well drop out of a world that was dropping away from you.

The current trouble had started two years before. Sara had always liked the first rains of winter. They cleaned the smoggy air and brought tiny green sprouts out of the summer-baked clay. But that fall the air never cleared and the dust never metamorphosed into fertile mud. Thanksgiving, Christmas, and New Year's Day passed with hardly a shower. Sara tried to help her mother keep the small winter vegetable garden watered, but they both grew discouraged; the broccoli was spindly and the lettuce withered. She wouldn't have paid much attention to what was going on in the rest of the country, but Diana, who still bothered to read newspapers, kept her informed.

While California's great central valley lay dry in the chilly sunlight, the farm states of the Midwest, blanketed by only the thinnest of snows, shifted uneasily into a rainless spring. In the East, late spring frosts were followed by hot dry winds that brought no moisture.

By the second winter of drought, lack of snow in the mountains and lack of rain on the western slopes of the Sierra watershed exposed the striated banks of rivers fed in other years by mountain runoff. Big rivers turned to muddy streams; small ones dried to a trickle of sewage.

Most staples were still available, but prices had begun to move beyond the range of all but the most steadily employed. Sara's family began to spend more time cooking and baking, devising ways to stretch the food they could buy. By spring, there didn't seem to be enough food at any price, and the lack of water was creating other problems. The President released a statement expressing "confidence in the ability of the American people to see this thing through with optimism and self-discipline" and announcing the inauguration of an emergency energy conservation program.

Until the drought, use of power had been rationed to what was jokingly called "waltz time"—three-quarter use in terms of 1985 standard. But water was still essential to power. Transition to fuels that could not be consumed— sunlight and wind—had been slow and halting, deferred year after year, sacrificed to the economics of what had been done. And what had been done was nuclear. To con-

serve nuclear fuel, to last out the drought, the power ration
was cut from waltz time to half use. The cities were dark at
night, and because so many people could not afford to buy
enough food, the streets were more dangerous than they
had ever been before.

Sunny was looking at her curiously. "What is it? Do
you hear something?"

Sara returned to the present and to the sound of the
river. She understood that her memories had been showing
in her face and that she had frightened the younger woman.

"No. No, it's all right Sunny. I was just thinking we
should get moving and find a more sheltered place to camp
for the night."

They got back on the wagon and resumed their trek
south.

The new conservation system had lasted only a few
months. In the middle of the second dry summer the leak
was discovered in Indiana.

Sara's father had brought the news home one night.
Evacuation had come too late for thousands of people who
lived or worked near the nuclear plant. Hundreds had died
already. Sara wondered how she really felt about the people in Indiana. She was sorry, certainly, that they were
dying, but more than sorrow, she felt anger. Everything was
changing. Everything was going all wrong, and it wasn't
just the ordinary kind of wrong she was used to.

The leak was in a standard, regularly inspected nuclear
power plant. Somehow the standard system had broken
down, and somehow the inspection process had been
inadequate. Washington sent out teams of investigators.
Another small leak was found in Nevada, still another in
Georgia. Within three months every plant in the country

had been shut down. In other countries, too, newly consci-
entious inspections, spurred by the trouble in the States,
were revealing unsuspected flaws. Germany was first to
shut down its plants, then Russia, then Libya—Sara lost
track. Even Diana was concentrating on what was happening closest to home.

No one knew yet how many people and animals, how
much land and water, had been poisoned. The government
issued reassuring statements: most of the facilities had not
leaked. It was only a matter of time, a matter of keeping the
systems closed down until new storage methods could be
devised. And new inspection procedures.

During the third winter, gangs of thieves, well-organ-
ized and armed with rifles and shotguns, began to attack
food transports. They stopped trucks and emptied their
cargo into waiting vans, many of which were pulled by
horses, the heavy and useless engines removed to make
more room for food. Trains were boarded at sidings and
stripped of agricultural freight. But most people were
afraid to become criminals. They thought, like Sara's parents, that if they just held on, worked together, sacrificed,
they'd be all right.

Power rationing was extended, step by step, even to
essential industries. Dairy farmers who had rarely touched
a cow found themselves, when there was no power, reduced
to massive campaigns of hand milking. On days when the
machines didn't run there was no cheese, no butter, and the
milk sat souring in the dairies. Without electricity, without
stimulants, without enough feed, egg production began to
drop. The managers of agribusiness couldn't produce
enough without their fuel- and chemistry-dependent methods to feed three hundred million people.

Some of Sara's neighbors joined the gangs of increas-
ingly acceptable, even popular, pirates and rustlers of the
black market.

The government began fighting back by sending army

escorts with all food convoys and ended, in the fourth year, by putting all food transport under the authority of the armed forces. That made some difference; it added another middleman to the black market chain.

Women, finding themselves even more vulnerable than they had been in normally violent times, began to band together to protect themselves from the warlike conditions of rape, robbery, and kidnapping, and to form strong support networks based on self-defense.

Sara and Diana made some useful connections among these women, and Sara's parents became involved in a food network of their own. Everyone was doing it, or dying.

But there was more than hunger to contend with, and more than organized bandits warring against the food industries or local gangs of young men raping and robbing. There were refugees: marching, shouting mobs, straggling, pitiful collections of families, abandoning San Francisco, carrying their possessions on their backs, fighting among themselves, stealing from each other as they came streaming across the Bay Bridge heading east and north along the nearly empty freeways, spilling over into the city streets to battle with gangs of residents, spreading up into the hills, camping in the parks and living off the small animals they found there, raiding the homes of those who still had some food stashed away.

When the Golden Gate Bridge was closed off by an army of Marin County vigilantes, even more San Franciscans, diverted from going north along the coast, turned east to invade Oakland.

One day Sara looked out her living room window toward the Oakland hills and saw what looked like a dark cloud rising. It took her a moment to realize it was a cloud of smoke.

By the time the fire burned itself out, it had destroyed more than half the acreage of the East Bay's park land and more than three hundred homes. The choking, heavy smoke hung for days in the still dry air. Two weeks passed before the cause could be traced. The fire had started at a stable. A band of refugees had attacked the main buildings, chasing off or killing the people they found there. Then they butchered half a dozen horses, cooked and ate them in the stable yard, saddled the remaining horses, and rode away, leaving their cook fire burning.

Sara and Sunny found a place to cross the river just below a tiny, deserted, decaying town. The bridge itself was barely passable, its concrete railings crumbled and its surface buckled.

Once the barrier of the river was behind them, they felt much farther from Demeter than they had before. They could almost believe that they were the first people to travel this land, guiding their wagon over roads that were no more than trails, around woods that were becoming forests, across meadows that once had been cultivated fields. Even the animal life was sparse or at least shy of the noisy wagon. They saw a few rabbits and deer, several wild, once domesticated cats, and a small pack of dogs that veered sharply away from them and ran barking into the hills and out of sight.

They did see a symbol of former life—a rusted hulk of an automobile crouched on its fenders at the side of the road. Sunny jumped off the wagon to investigate. This was something new and interesting. Sara trailed behind her.

It was a tiny sedan. "Early nineties, Japanese make," Sara said. Its tires, even its wheels, were missing. The bumpers were gone, ripped from the body of the car. The windows had been smashed and its hoodless front end held a maze of rusty engine. Sunny stared down into it, wondering how it had worked.

"Wouldn't Calliope love to see this," she said. "How much do you know about it?"

"Not much. You'd have to ask Redwood. She could probably even draw you a diagram."

Sunny abandoned the motor and went around to the side of the car. She tugged at the door handle. It was stuck fast. So was the one on the other side. She crawled in through a window, sat in the driver's seat, and put her hands on the wheel. "Must have been quite a feeling, driving one of these."

Sara nodded shortly. "It was." Sunny pulled at a knob on the dashboard and it came away in her hand. She looked at it for a moment and stuck it in her pocket.

"Souvenir," she said.

On the morning of the ninth day they halted on a ridge and looked down at farmland, a scattering of small cottages, and a large old house. "Prepare to be a man," Sara said, deepening her voice.

Sunny laughed nervously. Her hands were shaking.

"No point in giving away information," Sara added. "Let's circle around and come in the other way, from the west."

They were a hundred yards from the edge of the fields when they saw horsemen coming to meet them, three of them, each carrying a different weapon: a bow, a shotgun, and an iron-studded club that looked like a medieval mace. They were followed by a fourth man, also on horseback, who appeared to be unarmed and wore a long yellow robe. The man with the bow waved his weapon at them when he was still a good ten yards away.

"Stop where you are!" he shouted. "Get down from the wagon. Show your weapons."

Sunny was pale, her jaw rigid. Sara felt sick. Oh, Joanna, she was thinking, I'm going to die here. But she controlled the panic that made her want to run, stepped down from the wagon seat, and laid their one rifle and her knife on the ground. Better to lose their weapons than risk a body search. Sunny took her knife from her waistband

and laid it beside Sara's. The armed men galloped up to them, stopping short and spraying dust in their faces. They coughed and wiped their mouths and eyes. The man in the yellow robe rode his horse at a walk, well behind the others.

"Is that all you have?" the bowman asked. They nodded yes, that was all, and still coughing, turned out their pockets. The knob Sunny had taken from the automobile fell to the ground.

The bowman handed his bow to one of his companions, picked up the rifle, and caressed it. "Do you have ammunition for this? Bullets?" he asked, almost greedily. Sara reached into the wagon, while the men watched alertly, and handed over the box of shells. He took it as if he'd never seen such a thing, opened it, and counted the contents wide-eyed.

"I'll take that, Bert. And the gun," the man in the yellow robe commanded. Bert gave him the objects eagerly, ducking his head in a kind of bow. "Thank you, Bert. Now, who are you two?" He was staring at the two women, who hoped that they were convincing as men.

"I'm Harry," Sara said quickly, responding to the man's obvious authority. "And this is Johnny." These were the names they'd invented early in the journey, resembling their own enough in sound so they'd respond to them without thinking.

"Are you merchants?"

Sara didn't like the way he said the word. She said "no" just as Sunny said "yes." The man in the robe glared at them and spoke sharply.

"Where do you come from and what are you doing here?" His hair was black and cut very short. He was clean-shaven and sallow.

"We come from the west, sir, and we're passing through." Sara hoped it was all right to pass through. "We'll be going north from here."

"Are you extra sons?"

She hesitated, trying to decide what the term might mean, especially for someone of her age. "Are you idiots?" His voice cracked with anger. "What is the name of your priest?"

Sara could feel sweat running down her sides. But this was no time to give up. "Dana."

"You must have come a very long way," he said sarcastically. "I don't know a priest by that name." He turned to his soldiers. "They're runaways. Put them safely away, and I'll send a runner to find out where they're from."

"We're not runaways," Sunny snapped, beginning to recover from her first fright and shock at seeing armed men. "Nor idiots. We're just tired, very tired. We've been traveling for weeks. Can we expect no hospitality?"

"You'll soon be on your way back to your landhold." He laughed shortly. "You'll get hospitality there." He gestured to the armed men. The one with the mace led the wagon horses while the other two, mounted, prodded Sara and Sunny, on foot, ahead of them.

They were taken to the largest house. It reminded Sunny of Angel and Diana's farmhouse, but it was much bigger, three stories high, made of wood, with ornate wooden decorations along the overhang of the roof. It needed painting on the outside, and inside, in the large dim entry hall, the walls were covered spottily with some kind of crude whitewash. But the old hardwood floors shone, reflecting furnishings that were much patched and repaired. The formal dining room contained a large, rough wooden table and a rug of plaited grass. They were taken through the dining room into the kitchen, which smelled of wood smoke, the walls showing the many not-very-successful attempts to scrub off the soot. The guards marched them through the kitchen to the cellar stairs.

"Go on, go down there," Bert told them. They descended to the dusty basement, Bert leading the way to a heavy door with a huge padlock hanging from the hasp. He took a ring of keys down from the wall and tried three of them before the lock fell open. The door creaked loudly when he opened it. "Get inside," he said grinning, "and make yourselves at home." They entered, and the door thudded shut after them.

They were in a room about twelve feet square. The only light and air came from one window criss-crossed with strands of wire. All the other windows were boarded up. The only furnishings were a filthy cot and a large, blackened, malodorous pot, the use for which they could only guess.

"Well, at least it's not damp," Sunny said.

"Beautiful old house, isn't it?" Sara said. "I always liked Victorians, but my mother said they were hard to keep clean."

"What are you babbling about?"

"I'm terrified."

"So am I." Sunny began to pace along the walls of the cellar, looking up at the boarded windows. "We have to get out of here." She turned to Sara. "That man was a priest, wasn't he?"

"He looks a lot like those priests we used to see, except his robe is clean. They were just a bunch of crazies. Fanatics." Sara shuddered.

"You think this one is sane? I couldn't understand a word he said. What's an extra son?" Sara shrugged helplessly. The language was new to her. "It's pretty obvious," Sunny continued, "that 'runaway' doesn't mean anything good. Didn't Donna use that word?"

"Yes. Her father told Bennett he'd kill him if priests came looking for him." Sara rubbed her eyes, trying hard to think. "I wonder why the priest was so sure we were runaways."

"I guess we said something wrong."

Sara sat down on the floor. "There's something medieval about all this." She gestured at the walls around them. "Even a dungeon."

Sunny was pacing again. "I wish I knew more about history. Maybe we could make some sense of it."

"Well, let's just assume the worst. What do you think about that window up there?" Sara pointed at the wire-covered opening. Sunny shook her head. It looked too small to crawl through even if they could pull away the wire. They both began moving systematically around the room, examining the walls.

"There might be a door that leads to another part of the basement," Sara said. "This room and the one we came through aren't big enough together to account for the whole foundation. It's a big house."

"You're right. And here it is." Sunny was standing at the far end of the room, near some cluttered storage shelves. "Behind all this junk."

The light from the window was suddenly blotted out. "Having a little look around, boys?" It was Bert, peering in the window at them. "I'll be checking on you every so often. Remember that." He laughed and moved away, and once again they could see their gray surroundings. They waited a few minutes, then Sara joined Sunny at the blocked door.

"Sometimes there was an outdoor entrance to the basement, too," Sara said. "This has to be the way to get to it."

"Yellow Robe said he was sending runners to find out about us. If he really meant runners, it ought to take some time, but we don't know how much." They didn't know how often the guard would be looking in on them either, and although Sara wanted to get to work on the door right away, they agreed that it would be safer to establish the guard's routine first.

"That bed gives me an idea," Sara said, pointing at the cot. She went to the open window and shouted up to it, "Hey, Bert! Hey!" There was no answer. She shouted again, and they heard him running heavily toward the window. He looked down at them, frowning.

65

"Don't yell that way, or we'll have to shut you up. Landholder doesn't like noise."

"Landholder? I thought Yellow Robe was a priest," Sara said.

"Certainly he is, and that's not a funny joke. And you'd better not call him 'yellow robe,' either. You'll be fed soon, so shut up. And don't yell for me."

"We want our bedding from the wagon."

"There's a cot down there. Use it."

"It's dirty and probably crawling."

"So what? What are you, a pair of women?" He laughed, and left with another warning to "keep shut up."

"He was nearby," Sara said, "but not very. He didn't hear the first shout, or it took him a while to get here after he heard it."

"At least he isn't just standing there, right outside. So wanting clean bedding makes us 'women' . . . we'll have to watch what we say." Sunny pulled several planks of half-rotted scrap wood down from the storage shelves. "If we want to lie down we can put these on the floor." She laid the wood down and cocked her head at Sara. "This is all really amazing, isn't it?" Sara grinned weakly back at her, then turned sharply toward the door as they heard someone coming down the cellar stairs.

"You men in there!" a woman's voice called out.

Sara made her voice harsh. "What do you want, woman?" She nudged Sunny in the ribs and whispered, "Pretty good, huh?" She had decided to enjoy what she could.

"I've got your food. I'm putting it through the slot now, so catch it." A small panel in the door swung open and the edge of a plate appeared.

"You hold it there until we come to get it," Sunny ordered. The woman on the other side of the door was silent, but she held the dish part way through the slot until Sara took it from her hand.

66

"Where's the other one?" Sunny growled.

"It's coming, it's coming." Sunny took the second plate.

"Will you be bringing us all our food?" Sara wanted to know.

"Mostly."

"What's your name?"

The woman hesitated. "Why do you want to know?"

"So we can call you something."

There was suspicion in the disembodied voice. "Why?"

Sara and Sunny looked at each other, shaking their heads. "Never mind," Sunny said. "Go away."

Obediently, the woman went back up the stairs.

"She takes orders well," Sunny said.

"Awfully well. What is this stuff?" Sara picked through the food on her plate, then took it under the window where she could see it better. "Some kind of mush and some vegetables. Looks all right." She put a finger in it and raised her finger to her mouth. "Tastes all right."

They ate nervously, wondering if they should, and returned to the door hidden behind the shelves. "We have to find out where the horses are kept," Sara said, grunting as she moved a box full of rusty hinges, screws, and odds and ends to one side of the shelf. "I didn't notice any stable when we came in."

Crate by crate, one pile of debris after another, they slowly cleared away the center shelf.

"We'll just have to steal whatever we can get hold of. We probably won't find our horses again, and we can't escape with the wagon," Sunny said. "Look here!" They had uncovered a padlock and hasp, heavy, old, and caked with rust, on their side of the door. "Silly way to try to keep someone in," she gloated.

"We don't know what's on the other side," Sara reminded her. She began to work on the hasp, trying to turn the screws with a scrap of metal. "They're rusted to the hasp. Solid. We'll have to pull the whole thing out of the wood."

They were startled again by the heavy sound of feet on the kitchen stairs and quickly shoved some of the junk back in place on the shelf. They heard the lock pulled away and the door banged open by a guard they hadn't seen before. He shoved another man in the door. The man fell to his knees, and the guard, without looking at the two other prisoners, slammed the door shut and went back upstairs. Seeing that he had companions in the cellar, the man glared at them and slumped down against a wall.

VII

    For two days after Sara and Sunny left I avoided social contact, eating alone at home as much as I could, giving no one a chance to talk to me. But the night before the games, I decided it was time to rejoin the life of the village, before Athena got restive about my suspended head-measuring duties and my other friends began to feel obligated to drag me out of my retreat.

    I went to the dining hall and sat with Diana, Angel, Joanna, Redwood, Athena, and Firstborn. Bennett sat in his usual corner with the silent Donna. There were others at their table, but only Freedom appeared to be talking with Bennett, or trying to. When the two had first come to Demeter, nearly all of us had made some attempt at dinner conversation with them. Gradually, though, most of the women had given up, preferring the easy interchange with friends to Bennett's sulky monosyllables or, just as often, his boring monologs. Freedom alone continued to spend time with them. She often sat with them at meals.

Redwood nodded in their direction. "He's been trying to get Freedom to tell him where Sara and Sunny have gone. Why should he care about that?"

Angel, glancing at me, said quickly, "Oh, Bennett cares about everything that's none of his business."

"Freedom seems to be making him her business," Firstborn said archly.

Redwood swung around to stare at Firstborn. "She really dislikes him, you know." Firstborn arched her eyebrows and shrugged broadly enough to ensure that we would all notice. Redwood looked at her with distaste and continued eating.

"What are you trying to say, Firstborn?" I asked, wondering if I really wanted to hear her answer.

"Absolutely nothing," she said in a deliberately unconvincing manner.

"Then keep your eyebrows still," Redwood snarled.

"You brought it up," Firstborn said.

"Nyah, nyah, nyah," I muttered.

Athena smiled at my wit, which I thought was very kind, and said to Redwood gently, "She may be attracted to him, you know."

"That's disgusting."

"It is possible," Diana said.

"How?" Redwood was incensed. "I used a perfectly normal flower. And there's certainly nothing wrong with me!"

We laughed, but there was discomfort in our laughter. I wished someone would change the subject. I couldn't. I kept thinking of Freedom with Bennett, vague but disturbing thoughts. Athena ended the brief silence.

"Freedom's my friend. All of us are fascinated by him in one way or another. But nobody actually likes the man, and no one would allow the village to be hurt by him."

"She always did like animals," Redwood said.

Firstborn shrugged again, this time more subtly, and began to talk about the next day's games.

"Bennett says he might enter," I said. " 'Just for fun' was the way he put it."

Diana spoke sharply. "He won't be allowed in the archery competition. I wouldn't put a weapon in his hands."

Angel was watching Bennett. He had gotten up and was walking across the room toward the door, Donna trailing behind. "He looks strong," she said. "He should do well."

"He is strong. He fights well."

"Fights?" Diana looked at me, startled. "You've seen him fight?"

"I fought with him. He beat me. It was very strange, though. When I told him he couldn't beat me twice, he got very angry."

"Some men are like that." Redwood said it simply, but the old anger showed in the lines around her mouth. "Personally, I'd like to punch him." Athena and Angel smiled appreciatively; my mother looked serious. I liked the idea of punching him, but didn't admit it.

"Well, he's angry generally," I said. "He told me he wants to be in his own world."

"His world indeed," Angel grumbled. "His very own world."

"He's in ours now," Diana said smugly, as if to end the conversation.

I saw Luna enter the room. My mother saw her too, and beckoned to her. I stopped eating, watching her come toward us. Diana saw the look on my face and touched my shoulder. She looked disconcerted. Apparently it had not occurred to her that I would not have sought Luna's company. Briefly, under the table, I felt Athena touch my thigh.

"Hello," Luna said, catching my eye. She looked away quickly from my hostile frown. She did not sit.

"You worked in the clothing factory with Donna today,

didn't you, Luna?" my mother asked. "How is she doing?"
My mother was ad-libbing. I suspected that she had in-
tended to ask Luna about new settlement preparations, but
had been forced by my reaction to find a different subject.
Luna looked surprised by her question. I sneered inwardly.
Of course she was surprised. No one ever talked to her
about anything but her one area of expertise. She began to
chatter about Donna.

"Oh, she just sits there and does whatever you tell her
to do. She laughed once today, but she didn't talk much."
Luna looked around the table at everyone but me. Some of
the others nodded encouragingly at her. Firstborn was
watching me covertly. "When she does talk, she starts
nearly every sentence with 'Bennett says,' 'Bennett this or
that.' " She hesitated. Even she must have realized that her
observations added nothing new to our store of information about Donna. She began to sidle away from the table.
"I can tell you more about it later, Diana, if you'd like. I
promised to join some friends for dinner."

"Yes, certainly," Diana said, nodding too energeti-
cally. Luna left, and Diana turned to me. "You know, Morgan, I get to thinking about something and I forget about
everything else." She laughed at herself, but her eyes were
sad.

"It's okay, Mother," I said unconvincingly. I finished
my dinner and stood up to leave. "See you later."

As I walked away, I heard her say, "Oh, Angel . . ."

I was left with the rest of the evening. I wondered what
to do with it. I didn't want to go home and cry, but even
less did I want to go out looking for company, visiting
Calliope, or stopping by the Little Flower. I didn't feel like
looking for someone to talk to. I decided my emotions
would be safest at home. If I insisted on crying, I would do
it for a little while and then do something useful. Maybe I
could begin work on a play. A sad love story. I might as well

take advantage of what I was feeling and give it some purpose.

On my way home, I passed near the house where Bennett and Donna lived. I saw the group of children clustered around the door before I saw him, sitting on the step, and changed my course enough to pass closer than I needed to. He was speaking; he was saying something about "responsibility for the survival of the village." He stopped abruptly when he saw me and called out a greeting.

"Hey, Morgan, nice evening, isn't it?"

Cheerful, I thought, but not for my benefit. Nodding to his guard, who stood politely uninvolved perhaps thirty feet from the small gathering, I walked directly to where he sat, greeting the children by name. One of them, a twelve-year-old named Jana, was one of my brightest students, interested in everything and now, apparently, focusing her curiosity on Bennett. I asked Bennett what village he was talking about.

"My own," he said, smiling at me. "I was talking about how everybody works to make sure nobody goes hungry."

"Just like we do here," Jana said eagerly.

So, I thought, he was willing to talk—to the children. "Maybe you can tell us about the priests, Bennett."

A younger child spoke up. "They're like elders."

"Are they?" I answered sharply. "I got the impression that they had more power." I was remembering Donna's story and her father's fear of the priests. The children looked confused; they didn't understand.

"In a way they do." He was nervous, his voice hesitating. "But everyone has to belong to something."

"Belong?" I shot back at him, outraged at the implications of what he was saying. Jana began to fidget. She was apparently uncomfortable with the growing hostility between the two adults.

"I believe in what I grew up believing in. Just like you,"

Bennett said. "And I believe it's right to live the way I was taught to live."

"Just like me," I mocked. "What are you trying to do, anyway?" I indicated the children with a wave of my hand.

He flushed and stood up. "I didn't drag them here. They were hanging around waiting for me." Jana frowned. His explanation didn't leave her much dignity. "We'll talk about this again," he said to the children, entering the house and closing the door behind him. Jana was glaring at me.

"It was interesting what he was talking about," she said flatly, challenging me and what she saw as my rudeness. I had interfered with their conversation and ended it through my interference.

"What he believes is dangerous." I spoke haltingly. "To us. He thinks what we're doing is wrong, and he would try to stop us—even hurt us—if he could."

The child shook her head, defiant. "You stopped him from talking." The other children nodded solemnly, agreeing.

"He wasn't telling the whole truth. We don't know what he's leaving out, but we do know that his world is hard to understand because it's so different from ours." They were listening.

How could I make it clear to them? They knew a little of our history, but they were so young, and the stories were just stories. And I was tired and wanted to go home. "I just want to warn you. Be careful of him. Be careful of what he says. Will you do that?" They were still puzzled by my behavior, but they agreed that they would be careful. They walked away slowly. Jana looked back at me once. She looked worried.

I wondered if I should have done more. This was different from any concern we might have about Freedom, who was, after all, grown up and probably more cautious. Well, I had done what I could. Everyone had to grow up and learn on her own. And I had to go home and be alone and try to work.

The house was cold. I built a large fire and settled down at my desk. I took out a fresh piece of paper. The color of cream. The color of the skin on the insides of Sunny's thighs. I stared at the fire, then forced myself to look at the blank sheet again. It stayed blank. She had been so cool before she left—so busy during that last week and so distant when we said goodbye. What if she never made it back? What if she came back and left again for good? I wanted her to come back to me and stay. Wasn't it that simple? How could she leave me if she still loved me? Wasn't that important? I had been trying to understand, really trying. I couldn't. I couldn't understand because I would never have left her. So I sat there, not comprehending, trying to write, trying to think, trying not to think, trying not to stare at the fire because it made poetry in my mind, and I didn't want poetry because it would hurt. Briefly I considered going out after all. But I knew that if I did, if I ended my isolation, I would talk too much. My friends loved me, but I did not want to subject them to my self-pity. No, I was being too hard on myself. It wouldn't be self-pity, really, just a need to talk out the pain until there wasn't any more to talk about. I wanted to talk about it now, but my anger would sound ugly, and I was afraid of sounding ugly. So I went around and around in my confusion. It was almost funny. Maybe I could find the absurdity of my misery, create the humor that would pull me out of it. I tried, but I was failing at that, too, when someone knocked on the door.

"Who's there?" Not "Come in," a welcome to anyone, but a need to know first who it was, to prepare myself.

"Athena."

I invited her in. I was glad that it was Athena. She always made me feel warm. She kissed me on the cheek.

"I came to visit you, to see how you're doing."

"I'm doing all right," I lied. But I did feel better, with her there. I offered her some tea, and she followed me into the kitchen, sitting at the table and watching me as I filled the kettle and put it on the fire. While the water heated, I sat down with her.

"I haven't been measuring any heads for the last few days," I admitted.

"Oh, that's okay. Maybe you could do a few more this week. I think we've got Angel fooled. She told me she'd be interested in seeing the results of my study."

"And so she will," I said, laughing.

Athena studied my face for a moment before she smiled at me. "If you're not doing fine, Morgan, you don't have to say you are. But if you are, I'm glad." I didn't know what to say to that, so I said nothing, smiling back at her, feeling a little silly. "Are you sure you're not busy, working or something? I can come back another time."

"No! This is a perfect time. I was just staring around, wondering what to do next. Now you've solved my problem."

"Oh good," she said, laughing. "I've solved your problem." Again I felt silly. How could she make me feel foolish so easily? I was weaker than I thought these days. My discomfort must have been obvious. She reached across the table and took my hand. "I'm sorry. I wanted to see you, but now that I'm here I don't seem to know what to say. Be patient with me, all right, Morgan?"

"Of course." I was puzzled. I didn't understand. I was the one who was confused, wasn't I?

"Morgan, I want to know how you're feeling. It's important to me."

I looked down at her hands, both of them holding one of mine. "Well, I feel terrible most of the time," I laughed. "And I guess you know things were pretty bad before she left. But still I feel cut in half. I miss her. I can't think clearly, and I wish my hurt would just go away. That's all."

"Can I do anything to help?" Athena asked. I looked

at her, trying to see behind her eyes. But I couldn't look into her eyes without letting her see me more clearly than I wanted to be seen. My gaze dropped to her full mouth as she spoke again. "Morgan? Do you need to be held?"

"No, please." I didn't know where to look next. "Do you want to see me cry? I'm ugly when I cry. My nose runs and gets red and my eyes get puffy, and to tell you the truth, I'd rather you didn't see me that way."

I was almost laughing. She did laugh.

"Vanity," she said. "That's wonderful. You're going to be fine, soon." The kettle was boiling. I disengaged my hand and got up to make the tea. I felt her watching me.

"Let's go sit in front of the fire," I said. She nodded and took her cup. We sat side by side on the soft couch, neither of us speaking. She didn't touch me again. When the tea cooled enough to drink, we began to talk as we sipped.

"This is one of Angel's recipes, isn't it?" Athena said. Ordinary conversation. Good, I thought. Or was I disappointed?

"Yes. A newer version of one of Aunt Helen's basic herbal brews. A few more odds and ends thrown in for flavor, guaranteed to create no startling effects."

"Good old Aunt Helen," Athena said, smiling. "So versatile."

"That reminds me. How's the baby?"

She laughed, looking down at her flat stomach. "I guess she's in there somewhere." She leaned back, stretching her legs toward the fire, suddenly silent and thoughtful.

"Morgan?"

"Hm?"

She was shy, hesitant. "Morgan," she said again. "I like you very much." She was looking at her feet. "I'd like to see you often. I'd like to get to know you well."

"Oh. Well, that's—" What was I going to say, "That's nice?"

"I know you're still in love with Sunny and maybe things will work out between you, but I could be your friend. I could give you comfort and warmth."

I touched her arm. "Athena, I'd like to be your friend." She frowned. "As for the rest, I don't know. I wouldn't want to . . . what's the word . . . I don't know, exactly . . ." My mind was failing me.

"You don't want me to be a substitute while she's gone. I suppose I shouldn't have just come here and blurted this all out. I've frightened you. I should have visited you every day, unobtrusively, sneakily, worming my way into your confidence . . ." We both began to laugh, but I was afraid I'd hurt her feelings.

"You haven't frightened me." It wasn't true; she had. "You've been so good for me this evening. I don't want to take advantage of that. I like you, too. Oh, I don't know what I mean to say."

"Good. Then neither of us does."

"I just feel numb most of the time now, when I'm not feeling awful. Angry with Sunny, frightened for her, afraid of what will happen when she comes back. How can I know how I feel about anything?" I stopped, trying to think of some way to make myself clear. She was touching my hair. I was not feeling numb, nor was I feeling awful. I felt a small, involuntary smile beginning. This had to stop.

"Athena, please don't do that. I can't think. And I want to be able to think. I really care about you, and I don't want to make love with you so I can forget about Sunny and because you're here and you're warm and you smell good and I like you very much. It's not fair."

She took her hand from my hair. "So. You like me very much. That's a good start, especially if I smell good. I spent the day at the lake on fishing detail, so that's really something." We laughed, but she didn't move away from me and I didn't move away from her.

We sipped our now-cold tea. I searched for the grief

I'd been carrying and found it. But I let it go again and listened, almost peacefully, while she talked about other things. Mostly she talked about the child she was going to have. I was able to listen for a while and contribute sometimes, until the gently sedative tea began to work on my exhaustion. I didn't have to tell her. She saw it soon enough and got up to leave.

"You're tired. I'll come back again soon. Is that all right?"

I nodded. "I hope you will. Soon." I touched her face. She kissed me on the mouth, briefly and softly. We said good night.

I gave up trying to work. I wanted to feel whatever it was I was feeling because it felt good, and that was new. Apparently, I thought with some smugness, I was not a complete failure. But it was that very thought that sobered me. I realized my motive in avoiding my friends had not been the noble one I had rationalized. I was not trying to spare them. I was embarrassed by Sunny's treatment of me. And I would be even more humiliated if she left me for good. I would feel better, I realized, if Sunny died—preferably in some useless way. That would allow me the dignity of tragedy. Love was disgusting. I was disgusting. I certainly didn't deserve to feel good about Athena. I felt more alone than I had before Athena had come.

VIII

There is a saying in the village about winter and the games: it will always rain on games day if not the night before. The tradition dated back to the first year in the village, the day after the founders had finished clearing the field for the first time. They were eager for the games, but it had rained hard. They had run footraces anyway, in the mud and the rain. They never let us younger women forget it, either; if we could see through the downpour, we played or we faced their scorn.

And so it rained that night before the games, off and on, and I lay listening to it.

The first sun dried up most of the mud, but there were still slick, damp spots on the field when I arrived. The games had not yet begun; the grassy field was full of women and girls jogging, running in place, stretching their muscles in the morning chill, doing pushups, chasing each other in play. Those who wore clothing, perhaps half the women on the field, wore bright colors. I was wearing a shirt and shorts, which I would remove for the footrace and put back on again for wrestling. I felt less vulnerable in the rougher games if my skin was at least partially covered.

The first event of the day was the discus, a competition I never did very well at. Sunny was good, but she always came in third or fourth. Of course, she wouldn't be there to compete this time. The champion was Joanna, who had fashioned the disk in the first place, forty years before when she was learning to be a stonemason. She was rarely beaten, rarely even tied; still, nearly all of us gave it a try every month. In archery, Calliope, Redwood, and Joanna seemed to take turns winning. My own favorites were the footrace and volleyball. I did pretty well at softball and wrestling, but the softball had a permanent grudge against a once-sprained finger, and wrestling—well, I was good but I didn't have the endurance some of the other women had. Perhaps I hadn't played as hard as they when I was a child. I had always been rather bookish, although Angel, in her mothering way, had encouraged me to use my body strenuously. I was taught, as all of us were, that it was important to be strong and agile. The competition made it fun, created the motivation to strive and to improve, and taught the youngest girls about playing with others in a formalized way.

I looked over the playing field at the colors—the pink-bronze, the yellow-bronze, the brown and black bodies; the reds, yellows, and blues of clothing—and at the flowing, rushing, and tumbling movement. The vision and the sounds, the laughter and the shouting, were abstracted by my lack of sleep. Donna and Bennett were standing not far from me, also watching. Bennett was scowling and his face was flushed. Donna, half a pace behind him, hugged herself, head down.

"Well, Morgan," Bennett greeted me, "I'm glad to see that you're not naked." His tone was severe. He looked anxious, angry, uncomfortable, all at once.

I shrugged. "I'm cold. I haven't warmed up."

"I'm not taking off my clothes. And neither is Donna."

"You don't have to." I turned my gaze again to the field, squinting slightly to see the pattern rather than the individuals.

"They shouldn't do that," Bennett was saying. "They shouldn't do that with me here."

"We'll do as we always do, Bennett." Then, tired of his silly talk, I changed the subject, asking what events they had entered. Bennett had entered them all, Donna none.

"Come on, Donna," I told her. "At least you can play ball."

"I don't know how."

"It's really very simple. When you come up to bat, you hit the ball and run. Watch for a while. You'll get the idea. Can you run?" I tried not to sound as exasperated as I felt.

"She can run," Bennett said, laughing. "She just can't run very fast."

"Can you run, Donna?" I ignored him.

"I might hurt the baby."

"That's silly. Athena's wrestling today, and she's going to have a baby." I knew the instant I said it that I shouldn't have opened the subject in his presence.

He moved close to me and took my arm. "I've been meaning to ask you about that, Morgan, about the little girls. Where do they come from anyway?" His tone was casual. I ignored his question, ignored his hand on my arm, and continued to try to coax Donna to have a try at the games. I felt his fingers tighten painfully. "Come on—how do you have babies here? Have you got men hidden away somewhere, in some cave?"

"Let go of my arm." I spoke quietly.

He held my arm even tighter. I wrenched it from his hand. "There's nothing to know." I walked away. The discus was starting.

A strong fifteen-year-old, daughter of my first bed-sister, gave a creditable effort—within eight feet of Joanna's record. Calliope followed with her usual short throw. Her strength always seemed to be mostly in her mind, and now her attention was partly drawn to the sidelines, where Ocean was watching. I was third up, and although I was distracted by Bennett, who was staring at me intently, I beat Calliope by four feet. It would be an hour or more before everyone who wanted to gave it a try. I trotted off the field to where Redwood sat marking the tally sheet.

"When's Bennett up?"

"He's last. That's what he asked for."

I looked around, realizing suddenly that I hadn't seen my mother. "Where's Diana?"

"I don't know. I saw her about an hour ago down by the dairy. She was talking to Donna—until Bennett came and got her."

The dairy was at the far end of the village. When I arrived, Diana was still there, sitting on a milking stool, turning a pebble in her hands. I knew how well my mother loved the games; it wasn't like her to miss them. She looked up and smiled at me.

"What are you doing here, Morgan?"

I shrugged, kissed her on the cheek, and squatted beside her. "Redwood says you've been talking to Donna."

She nodded. "She's beginning to ask questions. I suppose that's good. It shows she's alive."

"About what?"

"The children, for one thing."

"Bennett thinks we have men hidden away somewhere," I said.

"Fine. Let him think that."

I told her about my conversation with him. She looked at the small bruise he'd left on my forearm. "He's very much alive, isn't he. Too bad." I hadn't heard her talk that way before. She saw that it shocked me a little and laughed and shook her head. "Do you know, he told Donna we probably want to use him as a stud. She doesn't much like the idea."

"I suppose not." The idea was almost funny. "You reassured her?"

"I tried to." Diana stood and picked up the stool she'd been sitting on, turning it upside down, pulling at one of its legs. "Loose," she muttered. "No one sees to things the way Sara does."

"Mother, that leg has been loose for months."

Diana looked at me sulkily, preferring her own truth to mine. She sighed, put the stool down again, right side up, sat on it, and glanced in the direction of the playing field. It couldn't be seen from where we were, but we could hear an occasional, particularly loud cheer. She returned to the subject of Bennett.

"It's such an impossible situation. I'm going to talk to the elders about it. We need to come up with some ideas."

"The elders? Why just the elders? What about the rest of us?"

"Don't be indignant. I just want to keep things quiet for a while. In fact," she said, looking at me gravely, "you might pass the word that we're not trying to keep anyone out of the decision-making process. Whatever solution we arrive at, we'll all have had a part in it."

"Then why a preliminary meeting—just to keep it quiet?" That seemed an unlikely reason. "And what about Sunny and Sara? Surely they'd want to be involved in any decision."

"We need a preliminary meeting because we need to discuss it among ourselves before we can even talk to you about it." I had heard that stubborn tone used before over less important issues. "We remember. We came from there. All the teaching of a lifetime can't make up for that experience." She paused, averting her face slightly. "As

84

for Sunny and Sara, they're not here. And it will be weeks . . ."

"All right, Mother," I said quickly, not wanting her to reconsider her delicate treatment of the subject and blurt out something I didn't want to hear. She was right, I thought bitterly. Why wait for someone who might not come back? "Let's go back to the games. You've already missed my monthly performance with the discus."

She laughed, but she didn't get up. She touched my arm to keep me there.

"Morgan, they shouldn't have gone. Not now. And the new settlement has to wait until we can deal with Bennett. I've spoken to Luna, but—"

"Oh Mother, it's no use." My voice shook. "Sunny— a lot of people think he's a reason for going, not for staying."

"Because he came here at all." She understood. Because more of them could come.

We were silent for a moment. It was too complicated and too emotional an issue for me. Everyone seemed to be using Bennett to prove her own point, to justify whatever it was she wanted to do. I took Diana's hand. "Come on. Let's go." She stood, still silent, and we walked back to the field together.

Angel was sitting with Firstborn. Diana joined them. I stayed for only a moment. I'd had enough of Firstborn's sly looks, and I didn't want to snarl at her in front of Angel, even though I was sure Angel knew how I felt about her daughter. I went to sit with Calliope and Ocean.

"Who's ahead?"

"Joanna. She just beat herself by two feet." Calliope yawned. "It'll be pretty boring from now on."

Ocean corrected her quietly. "Bennett hasn't thrown yet."

"No one can beat Joanna." Calliope sounded angry.

"For some reason, everyone thinks he's going to be so great at everything. Horses are big and muscular, too. I'd like to see one play softball." Ocean laughed and hugged her.

"That's true," I said, cheered by her attitude. "Sometimes we sound like the women our mothers told us about —the ones who thought men were better because so many of them were bigger than a lot of women. And because women got used to believing men were better. But he did beat me once at wrestling." They hadn't heard the story and insisted that I tell them about it.

"And he got angry? Sounds just like him." Calliope shook her head, then turned her attention to the field. "I think he's up next."

Bennett strode onto the field and stood still for a moment, looking at the crowd. He smiled and waved to Donna, who waved back. He took off his shirt, folded it carefully, and laid it on the ground. His performance was taking a great deal of time. I felt the impatience of the women around me. I, for one, was anxious to start the footrace. In my irritation, my attention wandered and for the first time that day I saw Athena, perhaps twenty feet from me. She was watching Bennett carefully, arms folded, eyes narrowed, yellow hair shining in the sun.

He moved into the throw, spun once, twice, and let go. A good toss. The heavy stone arched high and fell—maybe a winner. The crowd murmured and then was silent as the referee ran to the discus with her measuring tape. She shook her head and signaled that it was fourteen inches short, fourteen inches less than Joanna's. A wonderful performance. The crowd applauded. Bennett was frowning and pacing the distance. He asked for another measurement. He was shaking his head. I heard him say, "It's not right." The distance was measured again, and he still came up fourteen inches short. He stalked off the field. His guard for the day, seeing him move so rapidly, apparently intending to leave the games altogether, followed him.

I was disappointed when he didn't come back for the footrace, curious as I was to know if he was fast as well as strong.

I ran hard, but I was not in good form and ran a close third in a field of thirty-two, with Ocean second and Firstborn the winner. Athena came in eighth, and my mother, who had recently celebrated her sixtieth birthday, followed Athena in ninth place. I had wanted to win more than usual; I felt the need for it. Perhaps I would do better at wrestling.

Bennett came back in time for the wrestling matches. Dozens of pairs of contestants took their spaces around the field. Most of the women would be satisfied with winning two or three matches, feel that they'd done enough, and step off the field to watch the others. Sunny, once when we were first together, had fought and won nine matches, then collapsed laughing and exhausted in my arms. She had been the big winner that day. I had never gone more than five. When I was very small, I had seen my mother win thirteen times. She was beaten in the end by Sara, who had won fifteen.

I made it through two easy ones and, taking a moment to rest, noticed that Bennett was still on the field, eligible as a winner to try again. He approached me jauntily.

"You said you wanted to give it another try, Morgan."

"I do."

We circled each other. He lunged and pinned me. I broke the hold and threw him hard. Harder than necessary. He came right back at me, lunged and missed, falling behind me as I danced out of reach. I spun and went after him, but just as I got within reach, my left foot hit a patch of mud and I slipped and fell. He was on me instantly, pinned me and kept me down. Despite the dubious circumstances, he was declared the winner.

He smiled as he helped me up. "You did well, Morgan. Maybe we should try again some time. I like wrestling with you." He winked at me and strolled away, looking for another match; he found one with Athena, who challenged him. I saw him laugh at the challenge, and I saw her angry look at his laughter. She isn't very big and doesn't look nearly as strong as she is. I had seen her beat heavier women many times.

The match between them was a long one. Several other pairs of wrestlers stopped fighting to watch as woman and man circled, feinted, clashed, and fell to the ground together, rolling, each trying to pin the other. He had her down. She got up. He had her down again. She got her feet under him and pushed hard. He fell several feet away, flat on his back, coughing, struggling to catch his breath. She flung herself on him again, and again he threw her off. They stood then, unmoving, face to face, glaring at each other.

"Measure his head for him, Athena!" someone yelled. He flushed and Athena smiled, but they didn't take their eyes off each other. My heart was beating hard, as hers must have been; I was damp with sweat, as she was. I wanted very badly to see him beaten. I could feel the excitement of the women around me. Someone nearby growled, "Get him."

She crouched, waiting, and he went for her. She stepped suddenly to the side. He lost his balance and fell heavily. She was on him, dead weight. With a great effort, he pushed her off far enough to get his feet under him, but he wasn't fast enough. She pinned him again, and though he struggled and tried to trick her by alternately going limp and moving suddenly, she had him long enough for the count. At three, she jumped off and clear of him. But he lurched to his feet and went after her. A referee who tried to stop him was shoved aside, but several nearby contestants managed to head him off before he reached the bewildered, retreating Athena. One of them shoved him down in the mud. Once again I saw the familiar look of rage in his face, but he controlled himself.

"Sorry," he mumbled. Donna ran to him, but he ignored her. She followed him off to the sidelines.

I approached Athena. Several dark bruises were beginning to show on her arms and legs. "Feeling okay?"

She smiled. "Sure. What a match. He almost beat me."

"You fought beautifully. He seems to be almost winning a lot today." We laughed together. I felt like hugging her I was so pleased. I didn't.

"He'll do better when he learns a little strategy," she said generously. She was looking at me closely and I knew she was not thinking about Bennett. I liked the feeling, but it made me shy. "He's very strong," Athena said. "I would have told him so, but he didn't exactly give me the chance."

"Well, I just wanted to know if you were all right," I said crisply. I didn't quite turn away.

"Morgan?" She was smiling mischievously. "Are you my friend?"

"Of course I'm your friend." I would have shoved my hands casually into my pockets, a habit I'd picked up from Sunny, but my shorts didn't have pockets. I felt a little indignant. She was teasing me. I had years more experience at this sort of thing, and she was skillfully and deliberately manipulating my responses to her. I had always thought Athena was so sweet! I smiled uncertainly at her and began to move off sideways. She moved off with me, but apparently had decided to shift to her role of friend for a while.

Her face serious, she spoke abruptly. "What are we going to do about Bennett?"

"I don't know," I said, following her lead, realizing I was following her lead, half enjoying it and half resenting it. "Diana's talking about a meeting. She's very worried."

"So am I. You know how you feel before you come down with a bad cold or something?"

I understood what she meant. "Or when you're up on a ladder and you feel it begin to fall?" I said. She nodded. She looked scared, and I wanted to reassure her. "Well, we're bound to be anxious. But maybe with a little time he'll understand and be happy here."

She reached over and touched my cheek. "You're so dear. Do you really think he can do that?" I wanted to wipe the dirt smudges from her sad face. Instead, I fumbled with my shirt collar.

"I'm going to go play volleyball now," I said formally.

"Yes," she said with equal formality. "I think I'll go talk to Angel about this meeting. See you later." We separated, and I walked to the side of the field where the women were setting up the nets. Bennett was there with Donna.

"Where do you get all this equipment, anyway?" he wanted to know.

"We make it," I said shortly. "Are you two going to play?" His question was harmless enough, but I didn't want him asking me questions.

"No. I don't know how to play, and it doesn't look very interesting, anyway."

"What about you, Donna?"

"I don't know how to play, either."

I sighed, impatient. "All you have to do is hit the ball over the net." I was growing weary of both of them.

"I think," Donna said, "we'll just watch." I looked at her, startled. Bennett looked surprised too, and a little displeased, I thought, that she had spoken for them both —that she had spoken at all, probably.

"I'll play softball," he said. "Wait 'til you see me." He sounded like a small boastful child. "Of course, I haven't played for a long time, but when I was little—"

"I'm sure you were very good," I said.

He was irritated by the interruption, but continued his narration. "My father taught me how. I was a champion hitter—or at least I would have been, if there had been any teams." He stopped, struck by a new thought. "How long have you women been here, anyway?"

"Why?" More questions.

"Well, it's been years since I heard of anyone playing

ball—and I never heard of women doing it."

"I'm sure you haven't heard of everything." I was no longer concerned about holding either my temper or my tongue.

He brushed my rudeness aside. "Okay, don't tell me. It doesn't matter. But did you ever hear of the teams they used to have? When my father was a kid? Things sure were different. He used to tell me . . ." He began a long story about his father's world. I suppose I could have listened, could have tried harder to understand him, but I had heard about those times before, from my mother's perspective. I interrupted him again.

"That's great, Bennett. They're choosing teams now. See you later, okay?"

I played for only a short time. The game wasn't as much fun for me as it usually was. My mind was too full of Athena and Bennett and Sunny. During one fit of dreaming, the ball caught me full on the nose. I wasn't badly hurt, but I left the game and spent the rest of the afternoon walking by myself. My injured nose made it easier for me to cry, even though I wasn't sure, really, what I was crying about.

I heard later that Bennett was up at bat twice, once for a base hit and once, to his intense irritation, to strike out. He threw the bat after the third strike, nearly hitting someone, and was thrown out of the game.

IX

"Welcome," Sunny greeted the man lying against the cellar wall.

He barely looked up. "I heard about you two. You must be crazy, coming here."

Sunny squatted beside him. He shifted slightly to increase the distance between them. "Is it so much worse here than anywhere else?"

"No different from where you come from, I'm sure."

"Then why are we crazy?" Sara asked the sullen man.

"What do you call it? Running away and running right into the arms of another priest. Just stay away from me. I don't talk to fools."

"Come on, we're all you've got," Sara said jovially. "Why are you in here?"

The man sneered, then shrugged, deciding apparently that they were indeed all he had. "They caught me stealing extra food."

The two women appraised him carefully. Neither of them was an expert on the state of the human body. He was young, not quite twenty. He looked thin, but wiry and strong. His coppery skin was clear and his dark hair and eyes looked healthy. Sunny wished that Angel or Athena could get a look at him.

Sara asked the question first. "Don't you get enough to eat?"

"Of course I do! Everybody does!"

"Don't get angry. I just don't understand." Her placating tone seemed to soothe him.

"Landholder knows what extra food is for. Running away. I saw your wagon. You know all about that." He became conspiratorial. "I saw your gun, too. Your landholder must want to get that back."

"The gun is ours. And we're not runaways, we're extra sons." Sunny had decided that to be "extra" meant to be superfluous and therefore harmless.

He laughed. "I never heard of no extra son having a gun he didn't steal. Or all that food, either. Good quality stuff. Where'd you get it?"

Sara ignored the question. "What will they do to you for packing away food?"

"Landholder will tell me that tomorrow, I'm sure," he said wryly. "The usual, I suppose."

"You're brave about it," Sunny said. "In our part of the world they kill you for running away." Sara shot her an appreciative look. They were working well together.

He was surprised. "For the first time? Takes two to die here. No, I'll be in here for a while, and I'll go hungry for a while, and then I'll work with stones tied to my legs for as long as Landholder says. And I'll have to do a lot of praying and repenting." He said it dully, with acceptance. Standing, he scratched himself briskly in several places and crossed to the cot, sitting carefully, testing it, before he lay down. The light outside the win-dew was getting dimmer. "Time for sunset."

But he wasn't just referring to the time of day. They heard what sounded like a crowd gathering a short distance from the house. The two women remained silent, waiting for him to say more. He didn't. The shuffling feet and buzzing voices stilled.

"God, thank you for allowing me to work another day." It was the raised voice, still querulous, of the man in the yellow robe. The crowd repeated, softly, what he had said. Sara tried to pull herself up to the window, failed, and looked about the room for something to stand on. There was only the cot.

"Great God, who has saved me from hunger and fear, thank you for giving me food and safety." Again the crowd murmured its repetition.

"Let me move that cot over to the window," Sara told the prisoner.

"Great God, who has saved me from wandering and loss, thank you for giving me this place on earth where I may belong."

"It's just a sunset," the man said. "Leave me alone."

Sara went to the cot and stood over it, threateningly, as the crowd repeated what Yellow Robe had intoned. The man grumbled and stood. She and Sunny pulled the cot under the window. Sara climbed up on it, and Sunny climbed up beside her. The cot creaked and swayed, but held.

The man in the yellow robe was standing under a huge old oak, his arms raised. They couldn't see the size of the crowd, but what they could see was entirely male, shoulders bowed, heads bowed, standing in a semicircle around the priest-landholder.

"God the father of us all . . ."

"God the father of us all . . ."

"God who destroyed the evil of the time before . . ."

"God who destroyed the evil of the time before . . ."

"When priests of the devil blasphemed in your name . . ."

"When priests of the devil blasphemed in your name . . ."

"When men lost reverence and hope . . ."

"When men lost reverence and hope . . ."

"When women whored and strayed . . ."

Sunny's mouth was open, her eyes wide. She glanced at Sara, but Sara didn't return the look. The older woman's lips were drawn tightly together; her eyes were cold.

"Forgetting where their honor lay in serving man and priest and God . . ."

"Forgetting where their honor lay in serving man and priest and God . . ."

"When giant cities rotted in their shame . . ."

"When giant cities rotted in their shame . . ."

Sara shuddered. "Not a bad description," she whispered. She was trying hard to pay attention, but she was remembering again.

"When all the earth and the skies and the seas were vile . . ."

"When all the earth and the skies and the seas were vile . . ."

"God, who made me in his perfect image . . ."

"God, who made me in his perfect image . . ."

"God, who made the priest to rule the landhold . . ."

"God, who made the priest to rule the landhold . . ."

There wasn't any doubt now in Sara's mind that this priest was a direct heir of those she'd seen in the last days of the cities. And now he and his kind had real power.

"You are no longer allowed to leave the city," the bullhorn-amplified voice droned. "Stay in your homes. Martial law has been declared. Anyone found in the streets after dark will be shot." The truck, pulled by three sweating horses, contained half a dozen frightened, starved-looking soldiers.

"If the soldiers aren't killed first," Sara said, letting the thick curtain fall across the broken, partly boarded-up window.

Diana nodded. "Nice looking horses—three tickets out of here."

Or food, Sara thought, for those who lived on more immediate terms.

"I wish Joanna would get back," Sara said nervously. "I hate it when it's her turn to get the ration. She never comes straight back. She always wanders around asking questions and 'observing.'"

"She'll be all right." Diana sounded casual, reassuring, but Sara knew that she was worried too. The week before their neighbor had been killed on her way home from the distribution station, her food stolen. And besides Joanna, four more women who lived with them were out of the house on a weapons hunt. Diana lifted the curtain again, watching. It was a quiet day. Sometimes it was quiet in the city for days at a time now, the exhausted silence of a depleted population.

Sara's parents had been among the thousands who had fled to the country, hoping to find safety. They had tried to convince her to go with them to the small farming community where her mother had family. Sara had refused.

"I'm staying here with my friends. With Joanna."

"Joanna! I'm ashamed of you!" her father shouted. "I'll make you go, just to get you away from her."

"You can't make me go. I'm stronger than you are."

He was enraged. "You're just imitating that Diana. I never liked her. Always so smart. I suppose she's got a girl friend, too?"

Sara sighed and said nothing.

"What happened to her parents, anyway?" her mother

wanted to know. "And what about the other girls, what about their families?"

"Dead," Sara said. "Or gone away like you're going."

"But you can't stay here," her mother said. "Just young women, alone, with all those men running wild."

"They think they can take care of themselves. They think they're better than men," her father said. His voice was angry but his face was sad. Sara felt torn, not wanting to lose them, but unable to go with them and live their way.

"I can't go with you, Daddy. You know that," she said softly.

And in the end they had given up and gone without her. It hadn't been long after that that the cities were "closed" by martial law. But the law could not be enforced. The soldiers couldn't keep people in or out of the cities, nor could they prevent or stop the riots and looting. Their own numbers were decimated by death and massive desertions.

So wanderers appeared and disappeared, carrying news and rumors—rumors of radiation poisoning, plague, cholera, and unidentified epidemics in unidentified locations. They came from isolated towns and villages depopulated by disease, crop failure, plagues of insects and rodents, and fear of being left alone in an alien wilderness. But they left again when they found the cities half-buried in their own debris, more populated by rats than by people, struggling to maintain an illusion of order. A few months into this fourth year, Oakland had launched an "official" rat-killing campaign, promising extra food as bounty. Sara, Joanna, and Diana had hunted rats, but when they brought them to the distribution center for their bounty there was no extra food. Sara heard later that some of the hunters had eaten the rats they'd caught.

Sara and her friends banded together in half a dozen houses which they turned into fortresses. Only Redwood traveled, and the tall Native American traveled with a purpose: to find a place where all of them could live. The others stayed, gathering supplies and weapons, picking up what information they could from those who passed through. Joanna, the observer, the asker of questions, was especially good at information-gathering, and her long absences were hard on Sara.

This time she was three hours in returning. Diana, still watching for her—Sara could not bear to—was the first to hear the chanting and see the mob half a block away. She called out to Sara and they both went outside, peeking through a hole in the fence, trying to hear.

There were eight men wearing long dirty robes of various colors. Two of them were carrying a woman, one holding her arms, the other her feet, swinging her as they walked. She was screaming. The men were chanting words that sounded like "Woman for sale."

Diana began to run for the gate.

Sara whirled and grabbed her. "What the hell do you think you're doing?"

"We've got to help her."

"We can't."

Diana was crying. "They're going to kill her!"

"Maybe someone harmless will buy her. Some man." Sara said unconvincingly. "I don't think they'd sell her to us."

"Bastards. Bastards . . ." The chanting was growing fainter. They heard a voice in the next yard.

"Shit," the voice said, and Joanna scrambled over the side fence. Another woman climbed over after her. "Did you see that?"

"We saw how it started," Joanna's companion said. "She was with some men . . ."

"Let's go into the house," Diana said.

They barred the door behind them.

"This is Angel," Joanna said, introducing the newcomer. "I found her wandering around with nowhere to go."

"I found you," Angel said.

"That's true. Well," Joanna sat down heavily on a scavenged chair that breathed shreds of plastic foam, "where Angel found me was down on Telegraph Avenue. There was this big mob on a street corner. I kept back from it, you know, but where I could see. There were these three people. Two men and a woman—*that* woman—the one you saw. They were standing on some steps, talking, yelling really. They said they were from the government and that it was forming again and everything was going to be all right. But they really had to yell, because everybody was yelling back. And then—"she paused for effect, "then some of those guys in robes showed up."

Angel interjected. "They call themselves priests, you know? They pushed through the crowd to the bottom of the steps and began to talk about saving people."

"And how the old way was evil," Joanna continued, "and these government men were evil and that government women were even more evil and unnatural and that's why everybody was hungry. That's when it started getting crazy. Last thing I saw was those three getting dragged down off the steps by the priests. People began to scatter. I heard screaming and I took off. I don't know what happened to the men who were with her."

"I took off with Joanna," Angel said.

"Oh, yes, and look what she's got."

Angel reached under her jacket and pulled out a newspaper. "It's the *New York Times.*"

"From what I hear," Joanna said, "it's the last one."

Angel spread the two-week-old paper out on a dusty, scarred table, displaying the front-page headlines about a riot in Washington and a large photograph of the President's helicopter taking off from the White House lawn. More than five thousand wanderers had converged on the capital and marched on the White House. Hastily gathered troops had tried to fight them off. When the three-day battle ended, four thousand troops and citizens were dead, and the government, including the President, had fled to secret hiding places from which, the last of the newspapers said, they would attempt to restore order.

"We'll have to save this," Diana said, "for history."

Later that afternoon, the four other members of the household returned, carrying a rifle they'd stolen from a deserting soldier who had, they said, "just kept on running."

"God, who gave me woman . . ."

Sara was looking at Sunny with despair.

"God, who gave me woman . . ."

"God, who gave me child . . ."

"God, who gave me child . . ."

"God, who took me from the wilderness and gave me truth . . ."

"God, who took me from the wilderness and gave me truth . . ."

"That I might serve the land that serves the priest who serves you, God . . ."

"Got it all covered, haven't they?" Sara whispered.

"Great Father, we thank you at this day's end, and commend to you our families and the labor of our bodies. Amen." The crowd of men repeated the last of the prayer. The priest's arms fell to his sides. The men bowed and went on their way, presumably home to their dinners.

"Any different from yours?" their fellow prisoner wanted to know.

"No," Sunny said. "No different from ours." The two women stepped down from the cot.

"Even where *you* come from?" He looked pointedly at Sara with her black skin.

100

"We come from the same place," she said, indicating Sunny.

"Don't see many folks your color around here."

"Sorry to hear that," she said sarcastically. Sunny snorted. He looked at them suspiciously, not understanding the joke but knowing there was one.

"Everyone's welcome here, of course," he said benevolently.

"Right," Sara said. "What's your name, anyway?"

"Walter, family name Marks, landhold Peter." The words ran together as though he'd been trained to say it all at once.

"Is that the name of this landhold—Peter?" Sara was reluctant to ask too many questions, but she knew she had to take some chances. "Is that the name of your landholder?"

He was looking at her quizzically. "Where do you come from with all your questions?"

"From the landhold of Dana, far to the east."

"Must be pretty far, not to know about landhold Peter," he sneered at her ignorance. "And not to know you don't call a priest by his name."

"Is landhold Peter a large one for these parts, then?" Sara pressed on, wondering if this tiny village, smaller even than Demeter, was really as important as he thought it was.

"The largest, Landholder says." The man seemed proud. "And all in just fifteen years. I was a baby when we came here. A starved baby."

"And you're never hungry now."

"No."

"Then why did you try to run away?"

"I don't know. My own land, I thought. I got restless. Landholder said I couldn't be a priest, and I got angry."

"I suppose you don't qualify as an extra son?" He looked at Sara as if she were insane. She asked another question quickly. "Why can't you be a priest?"

"He didn't tell me why. I asked and he said no. That's all. It doesn't matter. I'm going to sleep now. I didn't last night." He turned over to face the wall.

The women waited until he was snoring. When they were sure he was asleep, they returned to their door behind the shelves and worked quietly, prying at the hasp, whispering conjectures about what they'd learned. They had to work very slowly, for fear of waking Walter. They'd been at it for perhaps two tedious hours when they heard footsteps on the stairs again and the familiar female voice.

"Hey, you prisoners—your dinner's here." Walter sat up, rubbing his eyes groggily, and went to the door. He took the first plate passed through and sat again on the cot to eat. Two more were sent through the slot. The vegetables were different, the gruel was the same.

"Is this what you always eat?" Sara asked.

"This is food for people who can't work," he answered. "No meat if you don't need it." He said this last in a singsong voice, the kind one reserves for home truths.

"Do you have a family, Walter?" Sara wanted to know.

"What do you mean?" He spoke with his mouth full of gruel.

"A woman, a child . . ."

"No, not yet. I have to wait for her. She's too young still, only fourteen. There's no one free and closer to my age."

Sunny nodded wisely. "That's hard on a man." She was thinking that, although Demeter was larger than this village, she had often felt that she knew everyone too well.

"No, not so hard." He laughed. "Doesn't your landhold have any widows and the like?"

"Of course," Sara said contemptuously. "But even so, it's not the same."

"I think it's better. I'm in no hurry to pick up extra baggage."

"Sounds like you'd still like to run away."

He lifted his head from his plate, where he'd been shoveling in the food. He looked suspicious and frightened all at once. "I'm not running anywhere."

"Don't you want to get out of here?" Sara indicated the cellar with a sweep of her hand.

"Sure. And I will. But not to be dead." He looked at them with sudden intelligence. "You got something planned?"

"How could we plan anything?" Sunny asked sadly. "Look around you. How could we get out?"

"Maybe you found a door—like the one back of those shelves?" He looked sly. They tried not to react. "Barnes told me about it after he was in. Maybe you think it goes somewhere?"

Sara was quick to deny any knowledge of the door. "We hadn't seen it. Does it go anywhere?"

"Who knows? What difference does it make? I'm safer waiting here. I don't know about you." He laughed at them, but his laugh wasn't altogether unfriendly. "If you try to get away, I'll have to tell them or I'll pay for it."

Sara decided to take a chance. "Not if you come with us."

"You'd never get beyond the grounds." He was uncertain.

She pushed a little harder. "We can get away. But we can't do it unless you come, too."

"Tell me your plan, then I'll decide." He strolled over to the pot, unbuttoned his pants, and urinated, splashing on the floor. The sound stirred unease in Sara's own bladder. She hesitated, then decided to give it a try.

"I'd like to use that now, Walter, and in our landhold we don't watch each other doing such things."

"I never heard a rule like that. You must come from the other side of the world." But he turned toward the wall, nevertheless. Sara squatted over the pot, and just after she'd begun, he whirled and saw her there.

"A woman! And you?" He turned accusingly to Sunny. "You're a woman, too. You're both women, aren't you? It didn't feel right. You don't smell right. And the sound of that—" he pointed at the pot—"that wasn't right, either."

"You're just too smart for us, Walt," Sara said, hoping the flattery would save them. He gave no indication that he'd even heard.

"Look at you. Just look at you." He spoke with anger and disgust. "Trying to be men. I bet you escaped from that village, didn't you?"

"What village?" The women began to sweat, wondering what he knew.

"That village of women. We heard all about it, just a couple of years ago, not far to the west of here. A visiting priest told us. And he told us what happened to the women who were trying to be men."

They listened to him with growing horror. "What happened, Walter? What happened to the women?" Sara asked.

"They killed most of them, because they wouldn't stop fighting. They burned down their village and took the ones they caught back to the landhold. The priest said they were killed or captured, but you two got away, didn't you?"

"No," Sunny sobbed.

"Where did they take them?" Sara hissed.

"Hah!" he grunted, as though he would never tell. "You got away, but not for long. Women! Trying to be men." He began backing away from them toward the open window.

"We're not trying to be men." Sara moved closer to him. "We're only pretending to be men so we can travel more freely."

"Women don't travel. You've stolen yourselves from men and from your rightful priest. It's against the will of God!" He was shaking with anger and with shock at what they'd done. He turned and lurched toward the window, cupped his hands around his mouth and prepared to shout. Sara brought her hand down across the back of his neck. He fell, but got up again.

"Where did they take them?" she said, raising her hand.

"North. But there's nothing you can do about it." He rubbed his neck and ducked away from her, heading again for the window. She grabbed him, spun him around, and hit him across the throat. He fell, choking. Sunny stood watching, horrified.

"We don't want to kill you," Sunny said, almost pleading. "Don't make us kill you." He couldn't speak. He was kneeling on the dusty floor, clutching at his throat, still trying to shout for help but achieving only a low croak. Again he got to his feet and this time went for Sara.

"Help me, damn it," she rasped at Sunny, grabbing a stick of wood off the shelf. She hit him in the face. He fell heavily on his back, apparently unconscious. Sara tore a sleeve off her shirt and stuffed it in his mouth. Still Sunny didn't move. Sara looked at her, sudden sympathy softening her anger. Of course the younger woman was in shock. She didn't know anything about fighting for her life.

Sara spoke softly. "Come over here, Sunny, and help me. He may wake." She began to unbutton his shirt. Sunny moved stiffly to her side and forced herself to help Sara pull off his shirt. "We're going to tie him with it, Sunny. Tear it into three pieces." Sara was sitting on Walter, prepared to knock him out again if he came to. Sunny did as she was told and helped Sara bind him: hands together, feet together, hands tied to feet behind his back.

Sunny was trying not to cry with shame for her panic and her inability to act. Sara spoke gently to her. "You'd better learn how to fight." But she could not resist adding, "This is real, you know."

Resentment brought Sunny completely back to herself. "What's real is that we'd better get out of here." She went to the hidden door and began to work frantically at the hasp. "We have to get out tonight."

"We don't know where to find horses." Sara spoke shakily, feeling her own nerves give way now that the fight was over and Sunny was functioning again.

"During that service I think I saw what looked like stables over that way." Sunny pointed toward the back of the house. "What if this doesn't lead anywhere, Sara?"

"It will." They pried at the rusty metal, cutting deep into the wood with the scrap they'd found among the debris on the shelves. It was almost completely black in the cellar. They could barely see to work. Walter was still out when they heard footsteps approaching the window. Sunny rushed to the bound unconscious man and pushed him against the wall out of sight. Sara stood against the shelves. A dim light, candlelight, shone in the window.

"Is everything all right for the night, boys?" It was Bert.

"Why don't you let us sleep, Bert?" Sara rasped.

"Sleep sound. I'll be protecting you all night long." He snickered and walked away from the window. They heard his footsteps receding for a long time.

"He probably won't be back until morning," Sunny said. They returned to their work just as Walter regained consciousness and began to groan through his gag. "Good timing," she added.

After perhaps another half-hour's work, their hands bleeding and bruised, the screws came loose with a tearing, screeching sound. The door bumped inward, two inches only, to the backs of the shelves. Sara put her eye to the crack.

"Can't see anything." They began to clear the rest of the shelves. Walter was trying to shout, but all he could manage, injured and gagged as he was, were a few strangled groans. The shelves cleared, their contents spread along the window wall, they tried to move the structure away from the door. It was attached to the wall. They found the places where it was nailed to the wooden framework with some difficulty, having to feel their way. They were discouraged and weary. More prying to do. Sara was cursing softly. "A whole village. Murdered." They worked quickly, starting at every sound, and in less than another hour had pried the structure free of the wall. Straining, they pushed it slowly away from the door.

Sara pulled the door open and they stepped into darkness more complete than the darkness they'd left behind.

X

I was sitting in a tall tree, unlike any tree I'd ever seen, its smaller branches drooping with big yellow blossoms. I was singing to myself and mending a milking stool with a wobbly leg. Demeter, far below me, looked different: the houses were smaller and all looked alike, their roofs the color of the sky, their walls the color of dust.

"What are you doing up there?" an angry voice demanded from the ground. I looked down. It was a man. I knew it was Bennett, although it didn't look like him. I didn't answer. He began to shout at me. He hadn't really seen me, I thought; I was too far up. If I kept still he would go away. But he began to climb the tree. As he came closer, I realized I could no longer see the village. There was nothing below me but branches, and the man directly beneath me reaching for my dangling foot. I struck at his hand with the milking stool, but the leg I was holding came loose and the stool fell away. I began to climb toward the upper branches, until I saw that he was suddenly above me. What kind of trick was this? I was angry and continued to climb, faster. He looked frightened. He moved back, away from me, until the branch he was clinging to began to bend. And then he wasn't Bennett anymore. He was Luna. If I kept moving toward her, she would fall. I smiled and, still smiling, woke up.

The dream had given me an irrational sense of accomplishment and a good appetite. I went to breakfast cheerfully, meeting Ocean on her way out the dining hall door.

"What happened to you?" She grinned at me.

"Just a beautiful dream," I said.

"Anything you'd want to talk about?" She was still smiling, but her blue-green eyes were serious and penetrating. Dreams were a passion with Ocean. She collected them, classified them, and worried at them until she thought she understood what they meant. Occasionally, she got a little boring on the subject, but she was a good friend and I tolerated her mysticism. I agreed to let her add my dream to her collection. It would be fun to tell it to her. She was on her way to the stables, and I said I would meet her there after I had eaten breakfast and before I went on to a late-morning class I was teaching.

I ordered a large meal and carried it to a table where Joanna was sitting alone. We found it hard to talk to each other these days when we were both thinking a great deal about the same subject, the scouts, and we were both trying not to think of them. Our most ordinary conversations had great blank holes in them. But we were trying now to treat each other with the affection we'd always felt.

"You're looking cheerful this morning," she said. I was beginning to feel uncomfortable. If the leftover mood of my dream was making so obvious a difference in my appearance, I must have been a depressing sight lately.

"I feel good," I said heartily. "And you?"

"Terrific." She picked up her plate and cup and, smiling warmly, rose to leave. "See you later. Have to get to work." I believed her, finished my own breakfast, and went looking for Ocean, feeling virtuous because I had gotten through those moments with Joanna without depressing either of us and because I was now going to give Ocean a present of my dream.

I found her cleaning stalls and laying fresh straw. Working with her was a thirteen-year-old whom I knew to be a carpenter apprentice in training with Sara. Since she hadn't been invited to listen to our conversation—I found the part about Luna a little embarrassing—she continued to work as I related the dream to Ocean. Of course, she overheard.

Ocean was a bit disappointed, I could tell, because the dream was too obvious to be a challenge. But she thought it was funny. The child, on the other hand, looked upset.

"I don't understand why dreams are important," she blurted out. "They're not real." Surprised by her vehemence, we turned to look at her, questioningly. She knew she had interrupted us. In a kind of apology, she continued, more quietly. "Well, I get tired of it, that's all. Lately everyone's always talking about dreams. I suppose it's because Bennett came."

"What do you mean?" Ocean asked her.

"Everything's different. I hate it. Last night in the dorm Jana had a dream she killed someone—a man, she thought it was. It made her sick. It makes me sick."

Poor Jana, I thought. All of us, even the very young ones. . . .

"Dreams are real," Ocean was saying gently. "Even though sometimes they tell us things we don't want to know." The girl snorted, but her mouth was trembling. She took her shovel and went to another stall to work.

"We know what she's thinking about." Ocean looked at me. "What about you? Are you really planning to push Luna out of a tree? Or Bennett?"

I shrugged. "Both of them, I guess."

"You have to get them up there first."

"How?" I was only half joking.

"That's a practical problem. I operate only in the realm of the intuitive. I don't really *do* anything."

"I've noticed." I glanced around me at the dirty stall. She went for her pitchfork, and I ran out the door laughing. I headed for the chronicle to pick up the old newspaper I needed for class and to spend a leisurely hour with it before class started.

I was nearly there when I saw Bennett, striding along, fists and jaw clenched. He had an ugly red bruise on his cheekbone. Freedom was about twenty feet behind him, just keeping pace. She looked angry, too, but it was Bennett's bruise that interested me. It was like seeing a tangible result of my dream. Curious, I approached him.

"Hey, Bennett."

He kept on walking.

"What happened to your face?"

He stopped and turned to me. "Ask her," he said, pointing at Freedom. "My guard for today." I looked at Freedom. Following the custom we had established for Bennett's supervision, she had stopped some distance from us, not involving herself in his private conversation.

"I asked you."

"Look, Morgan, you know I'm not a rapist." I was stunned. This was a word out of history. It had never had any relevance in my life. I stared at him, waiting for him to go on. "I know you don't like me much, but we've talked quite a bit together, and I think you're fair about things, isn't that so?"

"What are you talking about?"

"I didn't do anything!"

"I didn't say you did!" I shouted back at him, exasperated.

"You know how she hangs around me, talks to me."

"Freedom?" I didn't like the way he was speaking of her.

"I just touched her. I thought she wanted me to. That's all I did. She got upset. She hit me. I don't know what she'll accuse me of . . ."

I called out to Freedom.

She came, looked at Bennett coolly, and turned her attention to me.

"Bennett's hysterical," I said. "Did he try to rape you?"

Freedom looked as startled by the word as I had been.

"I don't know what he was planning to do. He grabbed me. I think he was trying to kiss me. I hit him. That's all."

"You thought I was going to rape you," he accused.

"It never occurred to me," Freedom answered, glaring at him.

"Then just be sure you don't accuse me of it," he snarled.

She gave him a disgusted look and walked off some two dozen paces to resume her watching post. I started out again for the chronicle office. To my irritation, Bennett came along.

"You believe me, don't you, Morgan?"

"Don't you have some work to do?"

"I want to talk to you first. I don't want anybody to think—"

"Why don't you get off the subject? What makes you think your bad manners are so important?"

I ducked in the door of the chronicle. I knew he had been told it was off limits to him. That made it a sanctuary for me at the moment. He stayed outside. I went to the cabinet where the newspaper was kept and lifted it out.

The founders had brought the old *New York Times* with them to Demeter. It had to be handled carefully and removed from storage only for school. The edges were brown, the pages translucent with oily preservative. It was pressed between two pieces of thin wood strapped together with leather older than the village. I picked it up, case and all, and turned to find Bennett blocking the doorway.

"Move aside, Bennett."

"This is where you keep your records, isn't it?"

"Yes."

"And you do all the recording, don't you? That's some job."

"Yes. Please get out of my way."

He didn't move. "Must be interesting. I'd like to have a look."

"You can't. Are you going to move?" I didn't want to have to put the newspaper down and shove him out of my way. Maybe I could do it with one hand?

"I just want to talk to you, Morgan," he said softly, and rushed on before I could answer him. "I've decided I have to explain things to you women. I was trying to talk to Freedom, too. I thought maybe she was beginning to understand, but now . . ." He looked at me patronizingly. "Maybe I can make you see it, Morgan. You're probably smarter than most of the women or they wouldn't give you such an important job."

"Why don't you just stick to your original plan and forget about talking to any of us, Bennett?" My voice was harsh and loud in the little room. "We don't want to hear what you have to say. And that includes the children."

"Oh, does it?" he said, smirking. "They seem pretty interested. Besides, I think you're more afraid of what they'll say to me."

I shifted my weight from one foot to the other. The newspaper case was getting heavy. I could have put it down, but I was reluctant to let go of it. That would be admitting that I was willing to stand there and talk to him. "Get out of my way, Bennett," I said wearily.

He ignored me. "I know why you don't want me to find out anything about you. You're afraid that I'm right, and that if I know what's going on here I'll be able to convince you that I'm right. Not that I don't already know some of what's going on here." I waved my free hand at him, brushing away his words. He only grew more adamant. "You can't live this way. God won't let you. Where I come from—" Losing patience, I took a step toward him. He saw the anger in my face and changed his tone slightly. "I just want to help you. I want to show you what's right. You can't go against the whole world."

"We don't need your help, Bennett."

"You're afraid I'll get away and tell someone, aren't you? Freedom told me that. She said you were afraid of being discovered."

"That's right. And for good reason."

"I wouldn't tell anyone. I just want to see you living right. I like you, Morgan." He smiled, but it was a cold smile. "I'd like to see you living like a woman, in a proper way, taken care of. Maybe I found this place for a reason. Maybe I'm supposed to lead you all back to where you belong."

"We belong here."

His friendly, protective manner began to slip. "If the priests found this place you'd all be taken away to live as you should."

"We can fight."

"You'd lose. And be killed. You're not safe at all." His rising voice cut me free of my own patience. Why had I bothered to argue with this fool? I shifted the full weight of the newspaper case to my left arm and advanced on him.

"Get out of my way!" I shouted. "Now!" I shoved him hard with my free hand and he backed, stumbling, out the door.

"You'd better listen to me!" he screamed as I strode past him. "Somebody had better listen to me!" He was attracting stares from passing women. "Don't look at me, bitches," he snarled. "Look at yourselves." And then he walked away, his fists clenched tightly at his sides.

I was still angry when I reached the school. The children had already arrived. Jana was there, laughing and chattering with the others. I didn't have to worry about her, I reassured myself. She looked perfectly all right, and perhaps this morning's lesson would be helpful to her. I cleared my mind, trying to anticipate the questions the children would ask. I remembered the first time I saw the paper and didn't expect them to be any more frightened by its revelations than I had been. The world of the newspaper was gone. Of course, I thought, waiting for them to settle down, we had other things to be afraid of now. The children were looking curiously at the wooden case I had placed on the large table. They began to crowd around it expectantly.

I opened the case and spread the paper out carefully, asking them to try not to touch it. Some of them recognized what it was. They had heard about the newspaper from adults and from older children. They were explaining it to each other. A few of them began to read aloud from the darkened sheets, stumbling over unfamiliar words, and Jana, I saw, was reading quickly and silently to herself. But naturally enough, most of them, especially the younger ones, were drawn to the pictures, not the print. I let the chaos go on, knowing they would tire of it themselves and begin to demand some structure for the lesson once they had satisfied their initial curiosity.

A ten-year-old began to read from an article about a South American earthquake that had killed 10,000 people. She read well. The others quieted down and listened. I listened, too. I had never been able to conceive of such numbers. Even my mother admitted that the world she had been born to now seemed unreal, even impossible, to her. It wasn't surprising, then, that these children refused to believe there had been so many people killed, or even that so many people existed. I didn't try to convince them.

Their attention began to wander from the earthquake story and they returned to their scrutiny of the photographs. They were particularly fascinated by the many pictures of men.

"There weren't very many women then, were there?" one child wanted to know.

"Oh yes, there were," I said.

"Well, where are they, then?"

"They weren't in newspapers as much as men were," I began. She looked at me doubtfully, and I was preparing to explain more fully when she was distracted by the conversation of the other children. Delighted to have found something familiar to connect with the pages before them, something to relate to their own lives, they were comparing the men in the photographs with Bennett. But some of the clothing, they decided, was very peculiar and uncomfortable-looking, not at all like clothing that Bennett or anyone else would actually wear.

I had spread out the newspaper in no particular order, so they came upon the front-page story only after examining advertisements and news that the editors had considered less important. Jana noticed it first: a very large photograph, surrounded by smaller ones, of a great many people running and fighting. The story was about a riot. They wanted to know what a riot was and did we ever have them in the village.

I thought carefully before I answered. "No," I told them, "we've never had a riot because there have never been that many of us angry about something at the same time."

"How many people does it take to make a riot?" Jana asked.

"I don't know. A few. Enough to make a lot of noise. A lot of violence. You've had fights with each other sometimes, haven't you?"

The girls giggled and looked at each other slyly.

"Well, just imagine a lot of people as angry as you were when you were fighting, only being angry not at each other but at something or someone else." They looked puzzled. "It's hard to explain," I said ruefully. "Maybe if we talk more about the riot in the newspaper you'll understand." They agreed that might help.

I explained carefully that the paper was very old and that the world they were reading about didn't exist in the same way anymore. All the disasters and riots and problems in the newspaper, I said, had led to the end of what then existed, including the newspaper itself.

"And it's all different now, out there. Where Bennett comes from," an eleven-year-old explained.

I nodded. "That's right. There was the world that ended before the founders came here, there's the world we've made for ourselves, and there's another world out there, changing and growing and becoming something new."

I read the story of the riot to them while they studied the photographs that went with it. It was a long article, but they listened intently while I told them how thousands of people had marched to Washington, the capital city, because they were hungry, and how the march had ended in violence and killing and the burning of government buildings. I added a little explanation of the word "government," drawing a comparison with our village council.

"What's this?" A child pointed to one of the photographs. It showed a helicopter flying away from the city. The caption said the President was in it. They wanted to know what a president was.

"It's hard to explain. A president was always a man, first of all, and he was a kind of elder."

"Bennett doesn't act like an elder," one of the children said.

"Well, maybe presidents were different." I suppressed a smile.

A child who had been looking at the picture with particular intensity wanted to know why we didn't have any flying machines. "Calliope or Redwood could build one, for sure."

"I'm sure they could," I agreed, "but I suppose they think we need other things more." The child looked doubtful and, I noticed, spent the rest of the discussion period dreaming and drawing pictures of flying machines.

When I thought their curiosity had been more or less satisfied about the events described in the newspaper and had promised to return to it another time, I led them into the subject of the chronicle, explaining why events are recorded. I told them we could have a newspaper of our own if we wanted to. They liked the idea and some of them began to talk about articles they would write.

Jana announced that she would write a story about Bennett. She said it as though she were challenging me, watching my reaction.

I reacted with irritation. "There are other things you can write about. You could ask Calliope about her plans for the new windmill. You could talk to one of the elders about how they first came to Demeter—Redwood has interesting stories to tell. You could ask Luna about the new settlement"—I made that suggestion reluctantly, but it stirred more interest than the others had—"or you can make up stories."

Jana's look told me what she thought of my ideas.

XI

Sunny began to move slowly around the walls in one direction, Sara in the other. The room was large, much larger than their cell had been. Sunny was first to find the outside door. "It's here all right," she said. "And locked. From the outside." Sara reached the door and pushed hard against it. "It won't open, Sara. I don't see how we can get it open."

They sat down on the cold concrete floor, their backs against the barrier door, trying to think what they could do next. Suddenly Sunny gripped Sara's arm.

"I feel a breeze, coming from over there."

They could see the dim outlines of a window. They moved closer to examine it. It was set six feet up in the wall and covered only with a fine mesh screen.

"It looks big enough," Sara said. "I wonder why it's so easy to get out of this prison of theirs."

"It wasn't all that easy, friend. Besides, if all their prisoners are like Walter, they don't have much to worry about." Sunny went back to their cell and retrieved some of the metal scraps they'd been using as tools. "We can cut through that screen with these. Climb up on my shoulders. We'll take turns cutting."

By the time they'd managed to break through, their shoulders ached and their legs were trembling. But they didn't stop to rest. Sara hoisted herself up to the window, peered both ways into the darkness, and crawled outside. She leaned back in, reaching down to Sunny, who found a toehold part way up the wall where the concrete had broken with age, and half-pulled her up and through the window. They crouched against the outer wall, resting, searching the dark. It was very quiet. They could see only one light on in the big house as they crept toward the back where Sunny had seen the stables.

They could hear the horses inside, smell the warm stable smells. The door was closed and latched with a long, heavy wooden bar. Sunny lifted the bar and the door swung outward, creaking, rusty on its hinges. They heard footsteps and darted inside.

"Someone out here?" It was Bert, speaking softly. The priest didn't like noise. They waited for him behind the door. This time Sunny didn't hesitate. When he stepped through, they launched themselves at him, throwing him to the ground. Sara gripped his throat, squeezing until he stopped thrashing.

"Is he alive? Sunny asked.

"I don't know. Who cares?" Sara spoke softly, but her voice was bitter. She was thinking of the lost village of women, of her own village, and of Joanna. "Help me strip him. We can trade his clothing for food. And he's got a knife."

"Too bad he isn't carrying his bow."

"I guess that's just for special occasions," Sara said. "By the way," she touched his throat and found a pulse, "he's alive." They took his boots and tied them in his outer clothing. While Sara went to get horses, Sunny gagged him and bound him with harness.

Sara came back triumphant. "I found our own horses, some rather nice saddles to go with them, and some water-bags. The wagon's out back, empty."

"I'm not surprised," Sunny said. They led the horses slowly and quietly out the door, across the dusty stable yard to the edge of a grassy field bordered by a line of trees. They hesitated, wondering whether to follow the trees for concealment or try for speed, cutting straight across the field. Sunny looked back toward the priest's house, still and dark. She was about to lead the way along the trees when she heard a door open at the rear of the house. It was too late to sneak away.

There was nothing to do but run. They mounted, urging the horses to a gallop across the grass.

Yards from the far edge of the field, they angled to the right to meet the road, their bodies bent low over the horses' necks, galloping harder and faster on the smoother surface, looking straight ahead, aiming for the rise. They raced up and over it. At the top, Sara slowed just enough to look back. All the lights were on in the priest's house, and she could see a dozen tiny figures dashing about the stable yard, gesticulating, some of them pointing at her. She turned and followed Sunny. The moon was rising, a bright half-moon that lit up the countryside.

At the bottom of the hill they stopped long enough to decide on their direction. They would go northwest to lay a false trail. Pushing the horses hard, as fast as they would go, they looked back only once more to see a mass of horsemen coming over the hill no more than half a mile behind them, none of them wearing a yellow robe.

The land stretched away on either side of the road, miles of gently rolling, moon-lit valley. Their road led to a low range of hills where they hoped they might find a place to hide and rest. They rode until the moon set. The horsemen were still behind them, though perhaps a little farther away. By dawn, their horses were faltering badly, and they slowed to a walk, looking as often to their rear as toward the hills ahead, catching sight from time to time of the priest's men in pursuit.

"They're still coming," Sunny said grimly.

"Not very fast."

"Do you think they'll keep on following us?"

"We'll keep going northwest until we know."

Sunny looked up at the hills. "Not much farther. I hope there's water there." She glanced at the empty water-bags they carried and patted her horse's neck. "We could keep going north anyway."

Sara sighed. She knew Sunny was thinking of the captured women. "Two of us? We'd just be caught ourselves. Maybe some day we can send an army of our own to rescue them."

The sun, still low in the sky, was warm. It was going to be a clear, hot day. Their throats were dry, and the horses, they knew, must be suffering. Sara's stomach growled loudly and Sunny laughed. Sara smiled back at her. "Funny."

"We're going to get away, friend," Sunny said.

Close to noon the horses, sweating and stumbling, began ascending the first gentle slope. The women were dizzy with thirst, the land wavering in the heat. Sara's head was throbbing and once she almost slipped from the saddle. They rode close together, touching often for encouragement and physical support. They didn't look back again until they'd reached the crest.

Far to the south they could just see the rise of hills that marked the perimeter of the landhold. They could see no one on the road and no dust cloud indicating riders hidden by a dip in the land, but the men could be resting, and they couldn't be sure they were no longer being followed. They stopped beneath a stand of scrubby trees. Sunny wiped blood from her cracked lips. The horses, exhausted as they were, wouldn't stand still. Their nostrils quivered. Her voice shaking with fatigue and fear, her mind fuzzy, Sunny spoke in a rasping voice. "They know something we don't. Let's take their advice." She gave her mare its head and Sara followed.

They smelled the green of growing things before they saw the crevasse, cut into the rock by a trickling stream. The banks were too steep for the horses, and they had to stake them to keep them from tumbling down to the water. Sara grabbed a waterbag and crawled down, scratching herself on brush and bruising herself on the rock, Sunny stumbling down after her and nearly rolling over her. They were laughing when they fell into the water.

"It's good," Sunny said, tasting, and stuck her head in, grazing her cheek on the bottom. They drank enough to wet their throats, filled the waterbags, and scrambled back up again to the horses. Sara poured the water into Sunny's cupped hands for the animals, over and over again, emptying the bags, sliding down the bank to refill them, and climbing back up again. When they finished watering the horses and had left them, staked, to graze, they took both waterbags back down again to fill for traveling.

Still no one was in sight. At their vantage point overlooking the road, they agreed to sleep in shifts, each for an hour or so. After much argument, Sara conceded; she would sleep first.

When she woke she looked at the sun. More than two hours had passed. Sunny ignored her angry glare and announced that she was going to sleep. Sara stationed herself to face down the slope to the road. About an hour into Sunny's nap she saw a dust cloud far back on the road and could just make out a tiny cluster of moving figures. They were going south, back toward their village. She suppressed a whoop of joy and let Sunny sleep.

"Guess what," she said when Sunny woke. "They've gone home." Sunny jumped up and dashed to the overlook, rubbing the sleep from her eyes. Sure enough, there they were going the other way. The two women stood hugging each other happily and watching the retreating dust. Sara was first to let go. "I still don't feel safe."

"I won't feel safe until we've been home for a week," Sunny sighed.

They turned southwest, heading again for the coast. It was two days before they found food in a corncrib belonging to an isolated farm. Raiding before the sun came up, they ate as much as they could and stuffed their tunics with dozens of ears. Sara wanted to refill their bags at the well, but Sunny, who had by now learned caution, convinced her that the well was dangerously close to the house.

Another day passed, half of it without water, when the horses carried them to a burned-out abandoned settlement near a small river. Ignoring the blackened wreckage around them, they headed for the well in the center of town. Sunny lowered the bucket and drew it up again too quickly, splashing some water on herself. Sara reached for the bucket, but Sunny stopped her.

"Smells funny." She sniffed at the water, tasted it, and spat it out again violently, jumping back on her horse and racing to the river, where she washed her mouth out repeatedly. Sara hovered over her, too distraught to drink, waiting. "Poison." Sunny sat back on her heels and wiped her mouth. "It has to be poison to taste like that." Forestalling Sara's question she added, "I'm all right and so's the river. Drink."

They sat on the riverbank, resting, watching the horses drink, each of them thinking about the poisoned well and wondering. Sara stood and turned to survey the ruins of the village. She had a growing, terrible suspicion. "Are you sure about that well? Who would do a thing like that?"

Sunny looked at her intently. "How can I be sure? I

never drank poison before. For that matter," she, too, was gazing at what had been a town, "who would burn a village? Steal pieces of it, perhaps, but burn it down?" She could see the remains of two dozen buildings, although there may originally have been more. Some of the blackened walls were nearly intact, leaning at odd angles, caved in on themselves, from corner posts and chimneys. Charred trees, dead and black, lined the main street, but the native grasses had come back, working their way through broken foundations and across paths. Like Sara, Sunny was remembering what Walter had said. It had been to the west, he'd told them. The village of women. They reached for each other's hand.

"Should we take a better look?" Sara asked, her voice wavering. "Maybe there's something—"

Sunny shook her head, beginning to cry. "There won't be anything to see. Besides, do you really want to know that much, and know it for sure?"

"No." Sara couldn't cry. Her whole body ached with the need to punish someone. "I want to get away from here now." She didn't express her next irrational thought: "Before they get us, too." They rode for half a day before they could bring themselves to stop and rest again. Sunny dozed, but Sara could not sleep. She was thinking that Demeter had been lucky all these years, that she and her friends had chosen a good place to settle.

The drought finally ended, late in the fifth year when it no longer mattered. It was during that fifth year that Redwood found a valley, a valley with a little town, land that had once been cultivated, and a clean and living lake, just outside the rim of the hills, fed by a stream that came down from the mountains to the east. It was deserted now and far off the main roads.

The network of friends, lovers, and friends of friends

began planning their migration. The women, nearly fifty of
them, would travel in small inconspicuous groups by a variety of horse-drawn vehicles and would rendezvous at three
points en route. The first meeting place was fifty miles
northeast of Napa, the second halfway to their destination,
and the third just a few miles outside the valley itself, where
all but two would establish a defensible camp. The two who
went on to the valley would reconnoiter, making sure the
place was still deserted.

Angel was looking at the map, following the route with
her finger. "This is perfect. It will take us right past a place
I want to stop."

"Stop?" Diana said. "We don't want to stop anywhere."

"Oh yes. We really should. It could be important to us
later on. There's a woman there . . ." Diana listened, nodding, as Angel explained, and agreed to help convince Sara
and Joanna, who would be sharing their wagon—one of
several that Sara and Redwood had built with materials
scavenged from the houses they'd been living in and from
the city streets.

Sara objected to Angel's plan.

"I want to get there and get on with it," she said.

"This is important, Sara," Diana explained. "There's
a woman Angel wants to see there, an herbalist. We'll need
medicines and salves and . . . things like that." Diana wasn't
sure of her subject, but if Angel said they should see the
woman, that was good enough for her. Angel knew about
such things. Joanna agreed that the stop would be worth-
while, and Sara, outnumbered, gave in.

Theirs was the first wagon to leave. They set out north
into Berkeley and from there followed Route 80 toward
Martinez and the bridge across the strait, planning to cross
at the bridge and go on into Napa County.

The city streets were deserted. The few people they
passed ran from the sight of their wagon. They saw aban-

doned cars and even an abandoned bus. The houses were open to the weather, their windows and doors broken or gone. Some of the houses themselves were gone, burned to the ground by either accident or arson. A side street was blocked by a barricade of felled trees. From behind the barricade a man screamed at them to "Keep out! Keep moving!"

They had nearly reached the bridge when a woman and man on horseback came galloping toward them. They looked terrified. Diana hailed them as they passed, but they didn't stop. The man yelled over his shoulder as they raced away, "Bandits, holding the bridge!" Joanna got down from the wagon.

"I'll go have a look." She wouldn't let anyone come with her, saying one woman might be inconspicuous but more than one would not be.

She came back quickly. "I saw them all right. They won't let anyone pass without payment. Heavy payment. They beat one man up because he had nothing to give, and he told me they took another man's wife. Some of them are wearing priest's robes."

Diana turned the wagon east. They would have to go the long way around and cross where they could.

Although their detour skirted populated areas, they were not alone on the road. They met travelers, all of them desperate, some of them dangerous. Most, half-dead with hunger and sickness, could be frightened off easily enough by the weapons the women carried. Sara was wounded slightly, on the arm, in a skirmish with a lone man who waved a meat cleaver at them and demanded their wagon. But only once, during the first stage of the journey, did they come close to dying for their wagonload of goods.

They had seen no other travelers for a full three days. Angel was sitting in the back of the wagon. Sara was driving. Diana and Joanna walked on either side, Joanna with a handgun, Diana with a hatchet. They were passing through a small wood when a band of five men on foot, armed with knives and axes, rushed from behind the trees and blocked the road in front of them.

"Where you women going with that wagon?" the apparent leader demanded. Angel, half-concealed by the crates and bags in the wagon, reached slowly down to where her rifle lay at her side.

"None of your business," Joanna said, raising her gun and pointing it at him. Sara held her hunting knife tightly in her hand. Diana raised her hatchet slightly.

"Get 'em!" the man spat, and they charged the wagon. The first went down with a rifle bullet in his head. Joanna shot one as he struggled with Diana, another as he dashed the knife from Sara's grip. Diana felled the fourth like a tree with two quick hatchet blows to the neck. The fifth had begun to run away when Angel got the rifle reloaded and dropped him as he ran. The women came out of it well, Diana with two small knife wounds, one in her side and one on her shoulder, and Sara with a badly sprained wrist. They did some fast doctoring and drove the wagon away from the scattered bodies of their attackers.

Above the mouth of the Sacramento River, they found a place to cross. Just as Joanna turned the wagon onto the bridge, Angel shouted to her to stop, pointing toward the water. She ran down under the bridge and out of sight. Joanna stayed with the wagon while the others went after Angel. They saw what she had only caught a glimpse of from the road: bodies, caught on the rocks, washed up on the bank. Only Angel looked closely at them. There were half a dozen children and adults.

"They've been in the water a while," Angel said, "but it doesn't look like there are any wounds." Good, Sara thought, keeping her head turned away. At least they weren't killed by bandits. "I guess people are just dumping their dead into the river," Angel concluded, straightening up and leading the others briskly back to the wagon.

They crossed the little bridge and turned west toward Napa. "Welcome to wine country," Sara said prematurely. She didn't think she would ever forget those bodies, tossed away like garbage. Fighting and killing was one thing, but those bodies represented a loss of hope.

It was not long before their wagon was rolling past field upon field where pampered grapevines had once stood in orderly and endless rows. Now they saw only dead vines and weeds and the rubble of seasons. Following Angel's complicated, second-hand directions, they found the herbalist's house at the end of a country road.

When they drove up, the place looked deserted. Angel called out. "Aunt Helen? Are you here?"

"She's your aunt?" Joanna asked.

"No, that's just what she's called."

Sara rolled her eyes. She still didn't like the idea of stopping before their first rendezvous with the other wagons, and she was determined to let the others see that she didn't like it. The front door opened slightly and a very old woman stuck her head out. "Women?" She hesitated. "You're not women bandits, are you?"

Angel reassured her and gave her the name of their mutual acquaintance. Aunt Helen invited them into her house and offered them a cup of tea. "I'd offer you something to eat, but . . ."

"Oh, no, no," Diana said. "We have food. We'll share it with you."

The thin old woman shook her head, about to refuse, but Angel spoke up.

"We need some of your remedies and preventives, Aunt Helen. We'll trade you food for them."

Together, they cooked a meal and sat down at the table. The old woman ate hungrily and then began to ask them questions about their destination. Although they didn't tell her where they were going, they explained that a lot of them were going there and were going to have their own village.

She looked shrewdly from one to the other of them. "Just women? What are you going to do about the future?"

Diana shrugged. "What about it? We may not even make it to where we're going."

"Oh, no. You have to think about the future. I can help you with that if you'll make me a promise. But that's business, not dinner talk. You stay here tonight, and in the morning I'll give you what you need."

Aunt Helen went to bed after dinner, and the four young women made their beds on the living room floor. They whispered together for a while, wondering what the herbalist was talking about, but they were very tired and fell asleep quickly.

In the morning, the old woman talked privately with Angel before presenting them with boxes of dried herbs and bags of seed, all carefully labeled. One bag of seeds she handed directly to Angel, with a sheet of handwritten instructions. She told her to "stick it in your pocket and remember your promise."

They gave her grain and potatoes and invited her to come along with them. She declined, but wished them good luck on their "expedition."

When they were well away from the house, Diana asked Angel what Helen had given her.

"And what was the promise?" Joanna wanted to know.

"I had to promise her we wouldn't tell anyone about those seeds she gave me. She's afraid she'll be killed if anyone finds out about them.

"Well, tell us!" Diana said.

"Oh, I think she's just gotten very old . . ." Joanna had stopped the wagon and they were all waiting for Angel to speak. "What she said was this. She found these flowers by accident one day when she was rooting around in the woods looking for mushrooms. She'd never seen any like it before. She dried the petals and made some tea. It tasted good." Angel was speaking rapidly, not looking at her audience. "She made some for her neighbors. They all got pregnant. With girls. Four women. And two of them didn't even have close male friends. She calls it the Demeter flower for that Greek goddess who was somebody's mother. That's what she told me."

"All right," Joanna laughed. "But the other herbs will be useful, won't they?"

"Of course!" They were all laughing.

Sara shook her head. "What can you expect from someone who calls herself Aunt Helen?"

Two days later they reached the first rendezvous point. Within twenty-four hours, twelve of the thirteen wagons had arrived. The women in the twelfth wagon reported that they were the last that would be coming. They had found the thirteenth wagon ransacked by the side of the road south of Napa and, lying near it, the violated body of one of the women it had carried.

The second leg of the journey took them to the halfway mark, to a place Redwood had found, an old children's camp beside a lake. They reached the lakeside rendezvous a day early, delayed by nothing more than beggars on the road. Angel had given away another sack of grain.

A few of the other wagons arrived before them. Some had had little trouble, but most had been forced to fight. Redwood's wagon arrived two days late, its cargo of scrap metal rattling against the sides of the converted truck, its passengers, Redwood and one other woman, gray and slow-moving with grief for the third in their party, the one who had died of knife wounds after a battle with bandits. Five days from the date of rendezvous passed, and still two wagons carrying seven women were missing. They waited four more days, then, group by group, wagon by wagon, they moved slowly away from the campsite.

XII

"Why just the elders?" Calliope wanted to know. "That doesn't seem right at all."

We had been sitting in the Little Flower after dinner, Calliope, Ocean, Athena, and I, playing poker—a game our mothers had taught us—when Luna had approached our table and asked if it were true that the elders were planning to hold a "Bennett meeting." I had told her carefully that, as far as I knew, it was so. Calliope, who was usually easygoing about anything that didn't concern her work, had objected vehemently.

"They can't make a decision about Bennett without the rest of us," she said.

"I want one card, Athena." Athena handed Ocean her draw card. "Isn't it just a council meeting?" Ocean asked. "I guess I don't know what's going on." She looked at her hand. The corners of her mouth tightened almost imperceptibly.

"If it is," Athena said, "nobody told me about it. As far as I know, none of the younger members of the council have been invited."

Luna, who had been standing, hovering, really, over the table, pulled a chair up and sat down abruptly, bumping the table and knocking over my pile of chips.

"Sorry, Morgan. Listen, they don't have that kind of authority, to call a meeting without the approval of the full council." Luna was a council member elected for the first time just the year before, and she had strong feelings about her political status in the village. "And you're right, Athena. I just heard about it myself from Freedom." I looked in the direction of the kitchen area, where one of Freedom's helpers was making tea for the patrons. Freedom was nowhere in sight.

Ocean was still looking at the cards in her hand, tapping her fingers impatiently. "Well, why don't you do something about it? Call a council meeting yourself, Luna."

"That's not good enough. The founders are meeting tomorrow. I could call an emergency council meeting for tonight, late as it is, but it wouldn't change anything. When it comes to a vote, they've got more members. They could vote that it's perfectly all right to hold a founders' meeting."

I objected. "I don't think they'd do that. You know perfectly well they don't always agree among themselves. If you told them how some of us feel about it, I'm sure they'd reconsider."

"I'm sure they'd reconsider!" she mocked. "Morgan, that's silly. They've already decided that's not what they want to do, and I don't want that decision legitimized by a council vote."

Ocean looked up from her cards with difficulty. "Luna, they're not the enemy. Isn't anyone going to open?"

Luna stared at her, angry. "What have you got there, a royal flush? This is important."

Ocean sighed and put her hand down on the table. "Can't we just finish this hand?"

"Luna's right," I said reluctantly. Calliope nodded. Ocean turned her cards face up. Four kings.

"Okay," she said in the voice of a martyr, "Let's talk about it."

"We have been talking about it," Luna said. "Okay, they're not the enemy. But they've got it in their heads that they want to meet without us. And it shouldn't be allowed. It's a bad precedent. Who called this meeting?"

"Diana." I felt odd, as though I were telling tales against my own mother.

"Then she's the one to talk to. Morgan, she's your mother. You go talk to her. We'll sit right here and wait for you."

"My mother!" I was incensed. "What does that have to do with anything?" I paused while a new thought took shape. "Are you sure everyone wants to come to this meeting? Whom are you speaking for?"

Luna shook her head impatiently. "I'm not speaking for anyone. The point is that they can't hold what amounts to a general meeting among themselves. Most of us aren't founders."

Athena, who had been sitting quietly while the rest of us argued, spoke up suddenly. "But isn't it only a preliminary meeting? Isn't that all right?"

"Not really," Calliope sighed. "There's never been a closed meeting before—at least I don't remember one." She looked at me for confirmation. I shook my head. There hadn't been. "And there shouldn't be one now. No matter what their reasons are. I guess you'd say it was the principle."

"My mother says that all the time," Athena said, smiling. I laughed. I could imagine Firstborn talking about "the principle," especially to her daughter.

But I agreed with Calliope. "It's true. Still, I think we

ought to talk to more people before we send any delegations to Diana or anyone else."

"How many?" Luna wanted to know.

"Oh, why don't we just crash the meeting?" I was startled to hear peaceful Ocean talking that way. I looked at her closely, but I couldn't tell whether she was serious or not.

"We may have to."

"Don't be dramatic, Luna. We won't have to. We just need to talk to people," I said.

"Morgan, you always want to talk. We have to do something."

The problem was that I needed more time to think. I wanted to hear what others had to say. I wanted to slow down the movement toward conflict. But I didn't think the founders should meet among themselves, either. Talking to the others had clarified my own discomfort, the doubt I had felt when I'd first heard Diana mention holding a meeting.

"Maybe we should just trust them more," Athena was saying. "It's only a preliminary meeting, after all."

Luna was impatient. "We don't know that. We don't know that they won't decide to go ahead and act without consulting anyone else." She stopped and looked up at the sound of the door opening. I looked, too. It was Freedom, walking toward us in a purposeful manner.

"There you all are," she said. She turned to Luna. "I've been over at the dining hall. We've been talking about the meeting—"

"That's a coincidence," Ocean said.

"What else would anybody be talking about?" Luna shot back.

Freedom continued, "Some of us think we should have a session of our own tonight. Anyone who wasn't invited to the founders' meeting." Freedom spoke in a clipped, efficient way. This was her issue. She was not about to let anyone decide anything about Bennett without her presence. "We've got about twenty women already and more should be coming. I'll go get them and bring them here."

"All right," I argued, "but give me a chance to talk to Diana first. Tell her what's going on."

"No." Luna was adamant. "Not first. We're going to get started now. Meanwhile, you can go and see her if you want to and come back here and tell us what happened."

I left the Flower and went looking for my mother. I found her with Angel at Joanna and Sara's house.

"Morgan—come in," Joanna welcomed me. The three of them had been sitting around the fire talking and drinking tea. Joanna offered me a cup, and I accepted it. My throat felt dry.

"Actually," I said, looking at my mother, "I came to talk to you, Diana. But it's even better that you're all here." All? Without Sara?

"What is it, Morgan?" Diana was businesslike.

"It's this closed meeting of yours." The words sounded harsh; I hadn't meant them to come out that way. But I continued without apology. "It's causing problems. Agitation."

"I was afraid of that," Joanna said. "Diana, I don't think it's a good idea."

My mother was silent for a moment, thinking. "Well then, what if we open it to the younger members of the council?"

I shook my head. "No. Not with all the founders. It's not enough. It's got to be an open meeting." Diana began to object, but I held up my hand to stop her. "I know you want to be cautious, but I don't fully understand why, and I don't think the reasons matter. Your caution is creating a division. We've always been one group before."

"The reasons are good, Morgan," Angel said.

"They can't be good enough. Mother, you said you felt the elders should talk it through together. Why can't you trust us to do it with you?"

"Perhaps if you understood more . . ."

"Tell me."

Diana settled back in the cushions of her chair and took a deep breath. "It's got to do with hatred. You know our reasons for coming here. It wasn't just an experiment in survival. We weren't 'getting back to nature' and away from a complex and oppressive society, although history had given us enough examples of that to model ourselves after. By the time we came here, there wasn't much left of that society or, for that matter, of nature. We came here to build something good, but we brought something bad with us. We were crusaders, in a way, reacting against what we felt to be the evils of the world. But our crusade was personal, too, and came from our own needs, from that world's attitudes toward us. You can't even begin to guess what it means to live in a world structured and owned by heterosexual males—white, heterosexual males at that. Three requirements for full membership. Lacking any of the three made life that much tougher. Lacking two out of three or, heaven help you, being non-male, non-heterosexual, and non-white—"

I was impatient and I let it show. I wanted to get back to the meeting at the Flower. "I understand all that."

"You do not! Every concession they ever granted was just that. Something they were willing to give up. Because they still had the power, and we were still asking to be allowed into the club. Asking! That's like asking a thief to please give you back your belongings. The society we came from had a thin layer of tolerance and justice stretched over it, but it never stretched far enough. And now even that's gone. Donna was sold to Bennett. Don't forget that. I thought some of our bitterness had worn away. It hasn't.

Bennett's coming has brought it all up again like a bad meal."

"I know all that!" I insisted, but I only goaded her into what looked like contempt for my knowledge.

"You didn't live it. I don't want you ever to have to live it. Any of you. Just let us meet once together and say all the ugly, hateful things we need to say, expose all the ugly emotions, the anger and the fear, to each other, to those who will really understand. Morgan, we need to work it out among ourselves before we can even begin to get down to considering reasonable action."

Her talk seemed ridiculous to me, but I continued to listen as patiently as I could. Her next statement made her meaning clearer.

"We want you to know our collective thoughts, but we don't feel there's any reason why our daughters should observe the process that leads to those thoughts. It won't be particularly enlightening, and it certainly won't help you to make any decisions."

She had her rationale all figured out and put into words. She was ashamed of what we would see. That understanding made me more tolerant of her stubbornness, but at the same time, I knew she would never have let me get away with this kind of doubletalk. I put it to her directly.

"You shouldn't be ashamed to show yourselves to us. I think we can be trusted to make our own judgments no matter how emotional you get. You're the one who taught me about ignorance, but you've tried to keep us ignorant of your feelings. I've felt your restraint—all of you—" I looked at the others in the room, "when you spoke of the time before you came here. Are you afraid we won't like you?" Joanna was nodding seriously at me but neither Diana nor Angel responded. "I'm sorry, Mother, but you don't have the right to have your meeting. I sympathize with your reasons for wanting it, but the younger women won't accept them. They're talking about it right now and I'm going back to their meeting when I leave here. They know I've come to see you. What do you want me to tell them?"

Joanna spoke first. "Tell them we'll all meet together."

"No," Diana objected. "Tell them to trust us."

Looking directly at my mother, who was not looking back at her, Angel said, "Tell them to make their own decision. But tell them what Diana has said."

I thanked Joanna for the tea and said goodbye.

I was shivering, partly from the evening's chill and partly from my encounter with Diana. It is not easy for me to argue with someone I love. But I felt that this once in her life her emotions were clouding her judgment.

Halfway back to the Little Flower, I heard the sound of light running footsteps coming up behind me and turned to see Redwood. She looked distressed.

"Have you seen Bennett?" She had guard duty that night. I shook my head. "Lost track of him. I don't know how—" Her voice rose in her anxiety.

I tried to calm her. "He can't be far. I'll help you find him." I didn't want to help her find him; I wanted to go to the Little Flower.

"Something else, Morgan." She gestured toward the hill where the goats grazed. "Firstborn says she thinks there's a goat missing. A kid."

"We'll find Bennett. Firstborn will find the kid." She nodded.

We were trotting past the woods when Redwood grabbed my arm and stopped me. She gestured for silence and cocked her head toward the trees. Then I heard a sound, the loud bleating of a kid. I hesitated, torn between catching the goat and searching for Bennett, but the next sounds sent me racing down the narrow woods path: children shouting and Bennett's deep roar of anger. I nearly stumbled over the tiny goat as it dashed, tangle-legged, past me on its way out of the woods. I stopped at the edge of the clearing, Redwood coming up behind me with the kid tucked safely under her arm.

No one noticed us. Bennett was surrounded by half a dozen children. Jana was among them. She was holding a knife.

"You were going to kill it, weren't you? With this!" She was shouting, waving the knife. "We saw you!"

"You kill animals!" Bennett yelled back at her, indignant.

"To eat. What are you doing it for?"

"For my child. For its health."

I noticed then a spot of blood on Redwood's shirt where she held the kid. There was a small nick in its throat.

"That's silly," another child said. "How does a dead goat make a child healthy? You can't feed a goat to a child that isn't born. You were just killing." She held a stick in her hand and moved in closer to the man. Jana moved closer, too.

"Not to feed him." Bennett backed away slightly, looking about him for another way out of the woods, a way not blocked by children. "It's a ceremony." His searching eyes found me and Redwood with the goat. His eyes locked on mine and a slight, sardonic smile twitched the corners of his mouth. "It's part of our religion, a custom. I'll explain it to you." He waited, expecting me to intercede, to stop the argument. I remained silent. The children remained tense, poised. Still looking directly at me, challenging me, he spoke again. "We do it so the child will be a healthy, strong boy." He had been thinking about the effect his statement would have on me, not on the children, and he wasn't prepared for the cries of shock and outrage it brought from them. "I would have eaten it afterwards," he protested, but the qualification didn't work. They had seen him trying to kill an animal that was, by our standards, too young to kill. He was not killing it to eat, but to prevent the birth of a girl.

140

To these children his act was senseless, cruel, and now, finally, an insult to all of them. The youngest child—she must have been about ten—picked up a rock and threw it at him. She missed.

"I hate you, Bennett!" she screamed, and the others began to run toward him, Jana still holding the knife.

"No!" I shouted. "Stop!" I was terrified. They didn't know what they were doing. I pushed my way through and shoved the enraged children back away from him. Some of them were crying. "The kid is safe," I said to Jana, shaking her. Startled out of her rage, she looked dazed. "Now all of you go, go home!" They ran out of the woods, leaving me with a sputtering Bennett and Redwood. The founder stood half-turned from me, absentmindedly stroking the goat's neck.

"Crazy little monsters," Bennett exclaimed. "What kind of girls would—she pushed me and ripped the knife right out of my hand." He was truly shocked by Jana's behavior.

I nodded approvingly. "She was brave to do that. And right." He glared at me. "You stole that animal and tried to kill it. We couldn't let the children punish you, but you'll pay somehow, Bennett."

Redwood took his arm with her free hand. He looked as though he were going to spit at her when she said, "You're going back to your house right now and you're going to stay there." But he went.

I had praised Jana to Bennett, but I felt sickened by the violence of the children. It would have been terrible for them afterwards, remembering, if we hadn't been there to stop them. I realized suddenly that Redwood had done nothing to help me. She had only watched, while the children tried to solve the Bennett problem for the whole village.

About forty women had gathered at the Flower by the time I got there. I told them what the three elders had said about their plans for a closed meeting, and I told them about the confrontation in the woods. They listened quietly. The decision had already been made, while I was busy saving Bennett's life. They had voted for an open meeting the following night.

XIII

"I wish I knew as much about plants as Angel does," Sara said, gazing despondently at the wild green spring growth of the land around them. "We could live on salad."

"We'll do all right as long as there are dandelions," Sunny said, but she was getting worried too. The corn they had stolen was nearly gone. They couldn't live on greens for long.

They were still traveling west, both of them struggling with a strong desire to turn around and go straight back to Demeter. Although they were little more than halfway to the coast they felt as though they'd been plodding along for months, worn down by their imprisonment and escape, the loss of their weapons and supplies, and most of all by their discovery of the destroyed village.

But there was the ocean to see. Sara's memories of it were nearly as vivid as Sunny's fantasies. And though they had seen some possible sites for the new settlement, they had found nothing as perfect as their home valley.

So they had to keep going. The land itself would have to supply their food and their weapons.

They had fashioned spears from two straight fir saplings and tipped them with metal from the priest's cellar, but they served as defensive weapons only. Neither one of them had ever used a spear until Bennett had arrived in Demeter with his. It would take more practice than they had time for to throw one well enough to be able to bring down an animal.

The loss of the rifle and ammunition, Sara felt, was a disaster. Demeter had possessed only a dozen guns, brought by the founders. They were kept cleaned and oiled, but the limited supply of ammunition kept them packed away for an emergency, taken out for only the most essential practice by those who were already experts. Those guns, along with perhaps two dozen bows copied from the one Calliope's mother had owned, made up the whole of Demeter's arsenal.

The food problem was solved temporarily when they came on a small river. The fish were not much bigger than minnows, but they could be eaten and they could be dried and carried in the now nearly-empty saddlebags. Sara made a net of willow branches and the shirt they had taken from the guard Bert. For two days they camped beside the river, fishing and curing their catch in the smoke of their fire.

Toward the end of the second day Sunny, wading in toward shore with the last few fish they planned to take, saw a large object floating toward them from upstream.

"Sara!" she called out. "What does that look like to you?"

"A dead cow." Sara was about to turn away from the sight, stopped, smiled, and shouted back, "Catch it, Sunny!" She splashed out into the stream to help.

Sunny was horrified. "We can't eat it."

"No." Sara was triumphant. "But maybe we can use it."

They dragged the bloated carcass to the bank, retching, and took turns butchering it, one retreating from the stink, one hacking away with the knife. They managed to get enough sinew for two good bowstrings.

The rest would be easy. She had once watched Joanna making arrowheads and had gotten a lecture on bow-making. Yew, fine-grained and flexible, was an ancient source of bow-wood in this part of the world. By the time they reached the coast, she was sure they would have their bows and at least a few arrows.

"How are we going to catch a bird to feather the arrows unless we have arrows for shooting at birds?" Sunny wanted to know.

"We'll find them," Sara said. "If we don't we'll use something else. We'll make do."

Their third morning at the river they were packing up to leave when they heard a wagon rattling along the road. Standing behind a huge, half-uprooted bay tree and peering over a low branch, they saw two men in a wagon full of sacks and boxes. As they watched, the men stopped their wagon, took some waterbags from behind the seat, and jumped to the ground. As far as the two women could tell they were unarmed.

"We could run," Sunny whispered. A wagon would never catch them.

"No." Sara was thinking about the wagon. Food. Maybe weapons. The men were coming toward their hiding place.

"Stop where you are," Sara said, stepping out from behind the tree, holding her spear threateningly. The men stopped and raised their arms. They glowered at her.

"Priest's protection," one of the men said flatly.

"What's that supposed to mean?" Sunny growled. The man was startled.

"It means that if you steal from us, you'll have to answer to landhold Burton. We're merchants. Burton's our main stop."

"If we kill you, we won't have to answer to anyone," Sara said in a low, deadly voice. The men didn't look surprised, not until Sara said, "We're not out to kill you. We're not bandits."

"Well, then . . ." one of the men said, dropping his arms.

"Put your hands back up." He did. "What's in the wagon?" Sara asked.

"I thought you said you weren't bandits."

"We're not. We're extra sons. But we've been robbed ourselves and we need supplies."

"We'll trade. What have you got?" The man's voice was still wary, but friendlier. He sounded hopeful.

"Not much," Sara said. "Some extra clothing and some fish."

"Keep the fish. We'll have a look at the clothing." He eyed the spear. "I'm sure we can come to some kind of peaceful arrangement. Names?"

"Harry. And this is Johnny." Sara was not sure about being peaceful. She wanted to steal the wagon.

"Sam." He thumbed his chest, then pointed to his younger companion. "This is my son Smith." Both men were dark and stocky, the father heavier-looking than the son. "We were hoping to stop here for a day or so."

"That's all right," Sunny said. "We're leaving today."

"Where from and where to?" Sam's tone was formal but light.

"From the southeast. Heading for the coast. Have some fish?"

Sam accepted the fish, broke it in half, and gave the other part of it to his son. "Thank you." He nibbled delicately at the minnow. "Don't know the southeast. It's not much traveled. We trade some coast towns."

Sara didn't respond to his lead, not willing to reveal anything more.

"You'll maybe find some women on the coast you can have."

"Have?" Sunny said.

"Sure. You know." He laughed. "Were you planning on farming and keeping house too?" Both men laughed loudly. The idea was obviously absurd. "But I guess you're pretty young, eh?" he grinned at Sunny, who was making an effort not to snarl back at him.

"There's some nice little hens on those farms out near the coast," Smith said seriously, "but you'll need to trade for them."

Sara hesitated. She thought they were still talking about women and decided to change the subject. "At the moment we need food. What have you got?"

Sam settled down to business. "Barley. Half a wagon of it. Some kitchen pots and bowls and the like. A few bags of dried beans. Let's see what you got."

They showed him the boots, pants, and jacket they'd taken from Bert.

"Nice saddles and blankets," Smith said, his attitude belittling the worth of the goods they were offering to trade.

"We're keeping those," Sara replied. He nodded.

It turned out that they were very interested in the boots, which seemed to be valuable, and they were willing to take the pants and jacket too. The trade was settled. Two twenty-pound sacks of barley, twenty pounds of beans, some salt, a battered aluminum pot that must have been very old, and two wooden bowls for the clothing.

"I've got a little bit of wine here," Sam said. "Let's have a drink on it." Sara and Sunny picked up their spears and accompanied the men back to their wagon, watching to make sure they pulled nothing more dangerous than wine from it.

Sam paused, his hand hovering over the wagon bed. "Look," he said. "I've got a gun right here. I can reach for it and shoot you before you can throw that thing." He glanced at the spear. "And I should. But if you're not bandits I don't want to. I want to make a fair trade and see you on your way. How about another trade? My boy stays here with the wagon and the gun and yours stays with him, with that spear. You and me, we go back and trade the goods and have a little wine on the deal. You've got a spear, I'm unarmed. We don't need your boots as much as you need our food. If you try something, my boy shoots yours. If my boy shoots your boy for no reason, you've got me. Fair?" Sara looked at her "boy." Sunny thought a moment and nodded. Sara and Sam between them carried the food and cookware back to the campsite. They sat down and Sam passed her the wine.

"You first," Sara said. He laughed and took a long swallow, holding his mouth open, dribbling a little, so she could see the wine going down.

"You two come from the same part of the world?" Sam asked sociably.

"No," Sara answered distractedly, still thinking of the wagon. "I come from a village farther east."

Sam stared at her and stood up slowly, clutching his wine. "Village? I thought you said you were extra sons. We don't want trouble."

"We are." Sara was beginning to understand why they'd been imprisoned and why Sam was frightened. At least she thought she was beginning to understand. "I don't come from a priest's village. Back where I come from they call two, three farms together a village. But they're farmers." Sam was listening, but he didn't sit down again. She stood too, and kept talking, hoping she was getting it right. "I don't know if it's exactly the same out here. We've got the villages and the people that belong to the villages and the priests, and we've got the farms. They pay in crops to the priests but they don't belong to them. And we've got merchants."

"Same here," Sam said, relaxing a little and handing her the wineskin. "And merchants are extra sons off the farms just like farmers are."

But the difference in the use of the word "village" was enough to make him nervous. Still standing, he drank and passed the wine to Sara one more time, then picked up the clothing they'd traded for. Sara escorted him back to the wagon. Smith and Sunny each took a swallow of wine, and the merchants climbed into their wagon, said goodbye, and headed north, no longer interested, it seemed, in camping by the river.

Sara and Sunny slung their supplies onto the mares and went off in the opposite direction.

They found their yew trees the next day and that night began to make their bows. They were camped on the edge of a young redwood forest, the straight, tall trees forming a stockade between them and the road.

"Must smell wonderful here," Sunny said with a grimace. "All I can smell is the fish in our saddlebags. In my hair. In my clothes . . ."

Sara laughed and scooped up a double handful of earth full of half-composted needles. "Here," she brought her hands up under Sunny's nose. "Stick your face in it. And let's not have any complaints about the fish."

"You stick your face in it, Sara. There's a snail crawling out of it." Sara looked down at her hands and walked over to a clump of fern, depositing the snail carefully under the plants.

Early the next morning, long before dawn, Sara woke with a start. Her face was damp with fog. The trees, close as they were, stood dream-like in the haze. She sniffed and sniffed again. She did smell it. She was sure she did.

"Sunny! Wake up." She jumped to her feet and began to shake Sunny, who in turn scrambled to her feet and stood ready to fight. "It's okay. Nothing's wrong."

"Then what is it?" Sunny was still frightened and cranky with sleep.

"The fog." Sunny looked around. "I can smell the ocean in it. Let's get started now. Maybe we'll get there today." Sunny was fully awake in seconds and even more excited than Sara. They started off in the dark. Late that day, they crossed what was left of U.S. 101. By sunset, they knew they were very close, probably less than twenty miles.

"We'll see it tomorrow afternoon," Sara promised.

They did. They had been traveling at a good pace over rolling hills for several hours. Through the morning, the fog had been heavy, cutting them off from their surroundings, stifling sound. Just after noon, the air began to get brighter, the sun burning through the thick haze. Sara said she thought she could hear the breakers. They topped a rise and there it was, fog lifting from its surface, gray in the cleft of hills perhaps two or three miles away. They could hear it for sure now. Sunny stopped and stared. The fog was dissipating quickly in the warm sunlight. While she watched, the sun broke through and the ocean began to shine.

An hour later they stood on a promontory overlooking endless water, blue and green and white.

"Well, there it is," Sara said as if she owned it. Sunny didn't want to speak at all. The promontory dropped away a few feet in front of them, down to the wave-battered rocks directly below. To their left, a drop nearly as sheer ended in broken rock and a wide white beach. Sara looked down the beach to its southern end and saw that there the land sloped gently down to the sand. She led the hypnotized Sunny back and along the top of the cliff wall until they found the path. Leading their horses, avoiding vicious tangles of wild blackberry, they made their way down to coarse dune grass, soothed the nervous horses, tethered them to a driftwood log, and walked down to the water.

"Is this seaweed?" Sunny stooped to pick up a long green bulbous object that ended in delicate ribbons. Sara nodded. "The white birds out there? Seagulls?" She pointed to a group of large, swooping, shrieking birds, some of which had begun to drop to the beach near them.

"Yes. They're probably wondering if we're food."

"I was wondering the same thing about them."

"I've never eaten one, but I've heard they don't taste too good. If we're lucky we'll find a dead one whose feathers we can steal."

"They're almost too arrogant to kill anyway. My mother used to talk about digging for mussels. What about that?" Sunny was more interested in food than in feathers.

Sara thought for a moment. "Too chancy. The coast was getting pretty dirty forty years ago. And I also remember something about a nuclear plant way up north somewhere . . ."

"The gulls look healthy. What's that, more snails?" Sunny splashed through a narrow channel of seawater to get a better look at the surface of a dripping rock almost covered in barnacles. But she was quickly bored with the small unmoving creatures and convinced Sara to walk down the beach along the edge of the water. Sara agreed reluctantly. This was all a lot of fun, but they were vulnerable down on the beach with the cliffs above them. Much too visible should anyone happen by. Still, this might be their last chance. She spotted something glittering on the sand and knelt to pick up a pale green piece of sea glass.

"Look here. This probably came from a coke bottle fifty years old." The glass was perfectly smooth and nearly circular, about an inch in diameter. Sara tucked it away, thinking she would save it and give it to Joanna. Sunny found and pocketed some bits of shell and a small twisted piece of driftwood with a hole worn through its center. The driftwood, especially, would make a good replacement for the automobile knob she had lost in the priest's village. As she was thinking how much Morgan would like the shell, she realized she hadn't thought of her in days.

They didn't find a dead gull, but they did find enough loose feathers stuck in the sand to make two arrows when they camped for the night. After several futile attempts with their spears they succeeded only in driving the birds away and had to give up trying to kill for more.

They decided to take a quick splash in the water before they headed back up to the road again. They stripped, both looking nervously up toward the cliff top, dashed into the water, and hurled themselves into a three-foot wave. That was enough for Sara.

"I could have a heart attack doing this!" She headed for shore. Sunny, gasping with cold and laughing with delight, followed her. They dressed quickly, grinning at each other. "But I guess it was worth the risk."

The ocean was bringing back childhood memories for Sara. She was getting eager, now that they were close, to see Mendocino again. They would go no farther south, although Sunny joked about visiting San Francisco.

"It just sits out there on this spit of land looking beautiful," she told Sunny, explaining that the town was just two hundred miles from San Francisco and had been tourist-favored.

Sunny looked skeptical. It had been a town. There was no reason to suppose it was anything but a ruin now. But when they spotted two small boats sailing close together a few hundred yards from shore, Sara insisted that they proved life along the coast hadn't changed much. She didn't want to believe it had and seemed almost dazed by her private optimism. She told Sunny of the vacations she and her parents had taken when there was still fuel and they could afford to buy enough to travel two hundred miles from home. These were pleasant memories and she was happy to share them with Sunny, who was surprised by Sara's loquaciousness. When they saw a large town in the distance, Sara knew it must be Fort Bragg. She remembered it as a town of 7,000 people, a mill town for the lumber industry.

They rode in cautiously, circling around to explore the residential areas before they braved the main street. They knew more about the social structure of the world now; they had dealt successfully with the merchants. But while their new knowledge protected them in one sense, it also made them fear, even more, exposure as women. They held their weapons ready. Sara still carried her spear. To Sunny, the better archer of the two, were entrusted the few arrows they'd been able to make on their way down the coast.

"I feel like Bennett riding into Demeter," Sunny said.

"We didn't let him ride into Demeter," Sara replied, her voice low.

Even the back streets were at first a great novelty to Sunny. So many streets. So many houses. But her wonder at the size of the town passed quickly. One street looked like another, colorless little neighborhoods with their shells of houses, many of them nearly roofless and tilted, rotting on their foundations, all of them stripped of everything that could be carried away. Even the native shrubs and grasses and the spring wildflowers encroaching everywhere on walks and lawns didn't help to alleviate the sense of desertion and death, nor to obscure the signs of vandalism and scavenging. The sight of a small skeleton lying in the gutter, which Sara assured Sunny was that of a dog, seemed appropriate here. They had been reluctant to go into the houses, although it would have been easy to do so with windows and doors and even whole walls missing. They were afraid of what they would find and certain there would be nothing left of the effects of the former residents.

They might not have stopped at all if they hadn't heard the noise. They were passing a small frame house, weathered gray by the sea air, when they heard a loud tearing sound followed by a crash and a shout. They slowed, listening, not knowing whether to gallop away or investigate.

"Didn't sound like a man's voice," Sara whispered. They dismounted and crept to the ruined door frame.

Two terrified young faces stared at them from the broken interior. Two young boys, one about twelve, the other perhaps a year older. One of them held an end of two-by-four he was pulling from the wall.

"What are you doing in here?" Sara asked, feeling aggressiveness was the proper approach to their obvious fear.

"Nothing." The older one spoke first.

"Are you from Mendo?" the younger blurted. He spoke the word with awe and fear. His older brother shoved him back and stood in front of him.

"They're not," he said. "Their clothes are the wrong color."

"We're strangers," Sunny said. "Extra sons. What's this Mendo?"

"We're not from Mendocino," Sara interjected, "but we're headed there. What about it?" The boys were edging toward a door at the back of the room.

"Don't try to run away," Sunny said, waving her bow. "I'll shoot you." She wondered if she could.

"We're not doing anything," the older boy said. "We live in Noyo. We're just looking around up here." Sara nodded. So the little town just below Fort Bragg still existed.

"You're not supposed to be here," Sara said gruffly. The expressions on their faces told her she was right. They were scavenging, apparently, on someone else's preserve.

"Don't tell," the younger boy said. His brother shot him a vicious look.

"We won't," Sunny said, "if you'll tell us some things." The boys narrowed their eyes and waited. "Like what's so scarey about Mendocino?"

"It's not scarey," the older boy answered unconvincingly. "They wear blue shirts, that's all, and they come to get fish from us sometimes. The priest's share. That's what we do. Fish."

"Mendo's a priest's village?" Sunny asked.

"You know that," he answered with an air of strained patience. "Everybody knows that." He was edging toward the door again.

"That's right," Sara said. "We knew that. We know the priest."

He hesitated, unsure whether to believe this incredible statement. "You said you wouldn't tell!"

"We won't," Sunny said. "Don't worry. Go on with whatever you were doing."

The boys fled.

"Well," Sunny told Sara, "at least they won't tell anyone they saw us."

"I don't know. I suspect it was the priest they didn't want us to tell. I'll bet they were just doing what everyone in their village does. Mendocino's a good ten miles down the coast. No matter what kind of rules this priest has and no matter how scared of him these people are, their need and his distance would make scavenging around here pretty attractive." She paused while they got back on their horses and continued riding toward the main street. "They might very well tell their people about us. That's why I said we knew the priest. I thought it might protect us."

Sunny was thoughtful. "But we caught them taking lumber. Their folks might want to kill us and dump our bodies in the ocean too. I think we should have a quick look around and start back east. No point in going farther south now, just so we can meet another priest. Of course," she said consolingly, "that means you won't get a chance to see Mendocino."

Sara laughed, a little sadly. Enough was enough. She didn't want to see Mendocino, not as a priest's village. More than anything, she wanted to see Demeter. "Well, you know, Sunny, I'm sorry you won't get a chance to see San Francisco." It was all a joke now anyway.

They saw larger buildings up ahead and the side street they had been traveling opened onto a wide strip. Off to the left was a long, high bridge. "Noyo's down below that bridge," Sara said. Directly across the road were some functional-looking buildings dwarfed by the huge, empty, once-paved area that surrounded them. "Lumber mill," Sara said, in answer to Sunny's questioning look. "That was a storage yard. The last time I saw it, it was full of redwood logs, six feet across, piled maybe two dozen high." Sunny shook her head, trying to imagine what it must have looked like. They turned north onto the main road. On either side were store fronts, motels, and other symbols of the past: banks, car lots, offices. Sunny was enthralled. Here was something to look at.

"Think there's anything left inside that motel?" Sunny wanted to know. She was looking at a large structure with two levels of rooms and an overgrown parking lot. The bulbs were long gone from the MOTEL sign, and the word, eroded by weather, was barely discernible.

"You want to look?" Sara said doubtfully.

Sunny nodded enthusiastically. "I remember Diana saying something about tacky motels, drive-ins, and supermarkets. She said for some reason, images of them kept cropping up in her mind whenever she thought of her childhood."

Sara nodded, smiling. "It was an interesting world."

They dismounted in front of the motel, Sara looking apprehensively down the street toward the bridge. No one was coming. "I'll stay out here and keep watch."

"You can't," Sunny objected. "I won't know what I'm looking at unless you're there to tell me."

"But those boys—"

"We must have at least a few minutes, even if they headed right home to tell about us." Sunny was pleading.

Sara shrugged. They led the horses past the motel office, its large front windows gaping empty. Not so much as a plastic chair inside. The courtyard beyond the office was overgrown with the ivy that had once climbed tamely up the walls. It had covered every surface, climbed the railings, and crept inside the open doorways of both levels of rooms. Sara and Sunny didn't see the swimming pool until they had almost walked into it. There was a scum of old rainwater on the bottom. The bare, cracked concrete, paint weathered completely away, showed in spots through the rampant vines.

They entered a room on the ground floor. It was empty, a bare cubicle with a few shreds of rotting carpet tacked to one side of the floor. They explored several more first floor rooms, Sara dashing out front to check the street every few minutes, but it wasn't until they'd gone up to the second level that they found an artifact.

Sara grinned lovingly at the plastic box. Its sides were broken in, its insides strewn around the room, and the glass of the screen lay shattered on the floor, but it was still recognizable as a television set. Sunny had heard a great deal about television and didn't have to ask what the object was. She examined it on her own, leaving Sara to her stupor of nostalgia. Sara didn't even notice when Sunny left the room. What she did notice was her own hand, reaching out, and she burst out laughing when she realized she'd been about to turn a knob. She was still laughing when she heard Sunny shout.

"People on foot coming this way!"

She raced out of the room and met Sunny, holding the horses, in the courtyard. They mounted and galloped out onto the street. There were people coming from the south; Sara didn't stop to see how many. They were close, and when an arrow clattered to the street in front of her horse, she knew there was no point in stopping to talk.

The two women rode north to the end of town, their

attackers far behind them, and turned east. They were three miles out of town before they slowed down.

"I guess it was a case of the second possibility," Sunny said.

Sara frowned. "What?"

"They wanted to dump us in the ocean."

Sara smiled. "Not so easy to do."

"No," Sunny said. "But I think it's time to go home."

XIV

The benches were already full when I arrived for the meeting. Even those who generally avoided public gatherings were reluctant to miss what promised to be un exciting show. After all, hadn't the founders wanted a closed meeting? I suspected that those who had come to see raving elders would probably be disappointed; I couldn't imagine many of the older women exposing unbridled and undignified passion in front of such a large audience.

The big double doors, front and back, and all the windows were thrown open. Those who couldn't squeeze inside the room could lean in the windows and hear and be heard. I looked for Jana. She was there, with several friends, standing against a side wall.

Half a dozen council members were talking among themselves at their table in the front of the room, farthest from the door. Diana and Angel were among them. They had both been members, elected every year, for as long as anyone could remember. Diana had been council speaker more often than anyone, even Sara.

I found standing space along a side wall just as Luna, the last of the council members, arrived with Calliope. They looked as though they were arguing. Calliope saw me, waved, and worked her way through the crowd. Luna came with her. We greeted each other and made a bit of small talk about the size of the gathering. I was glad to see Calliope there. I had heard she was on security that night, and security had become much more rigid since Bennett's aborted sacrifice of the goat the night before. The council had appointed Luna to reorganize and direct a more formal guard program.

"I was afraid you wouldn't be able to make it," I said to Calliope. "Is everything all right?"

Luna answered before Calliope could. "Of course," she said smugly, obviously pleased with her new responsibility. "We've set up hour-long shifts so none of us will have to miss the whole meeting." She looked around the room. "I expect this will take a few hours, anyway."

"How's Bennett doing?" Again I spoke to Calliope; again Luna answered first while Calliope just stood there quietly, chewing her lower lip, shifting restlessly from one foot to the other. I wondered what was on her mind.

"He's not doing very well," Luna was saying. "He's angry." I shrugged. This was nothing new. "Of course, one would think he'd be glad to be alive." She didn't look at me and she spoke casually, but along with her disdain for Bennett, I felt some disapproval directed at me. That wasn't new, either. Diana caught Luna's eye. It was time for her to join the others at the council table. I watched with relief as she strode away. How determined she was to be on speaking terms with me.

I looked quizzically at Calliope, and she answered my unspoken question. "Everyone's so excited in such a strange way. Bennett is enraged and terrified. He knows, or suspects. And I can't help it. I'm as excited as everyone else. I just want the tension to end. I want to be back in control."

Ocean, who had been standing near a window talking to some friends, came to join us as Diana stepped up to the dais and gaveled for silence. Talk settled down to a murmur as everyone made herself as comfortable as possible. Many of the women had brought cushions and set them on the floor.

"First of all," Diana began, "some of the council had a brief discussion before you all arrived and decided that Sunny must be commissioned when she returns to design an addition to this room." Nearly everyone laughed. Luna did not. Her expression clearly said, "What for?" Diana continued. "You know what we're here for. We need to discuss the problem of Bennett—and Donna—and take suggestions for solutions to that problem. Is anyone not clear about the issues?"

Angel raised her hand.

"Yes, Angel?"

"I think you should outline the situation for those who are less familiar with it."

Diana nodded briefly and began to speak, quickly, as though she wanted to get it over with. "I suppose everyone has heard what happened last night?" The answering murmur told her that everyone had. Many of the women turned, involuntarily, to look at Jana, who returned their look defiantly. "The issue is this: we have in our village someone who does not belong here. He doesn't want to live here, and we can't allow him to leave. He has tried to influence our children, and he has—by bringing incredible ugliness into their lives. He shows all the symptoms of a man raised in an extremely male-dominant culture. His relationship with the woman he considers to be his is offensive to all our principles. His presence is unbearable, but letting him go would be worse, because he would certainly betray us to the outside world—his world—and that would be the end of us." She paused. "Open to discussion."

Redwood, seated on a front bench near the dais with a large group of founders, raised her hand and was recognized. She stood and half-turned so she could address the crowd as well as the speaker. "Since he arrived, I've watched him closely. I recognize him. He's like the most egotistical of the males I used to know. I believe his existence is a great danger to us. The world he comes from is a great danger to us. I think he should be killed immediately."

The two front benches seemed to explode as a dozen or more founders rose from their seats shouting approval. Redwood raised a clenched fist in a gesture that had been old when she was growing up. They roared even louder, raising their fists, too. Redwood's daughter, Freedom, was standing next to Ocean, leaning against the open door. She was shaking her head violently, her eyes closed. She seemed to be saying something but I couldn't tell what it was. More women were shouting, some angry, some exuberant. Some were laughing. Ocean and Calliope reached for each other's hand. They were silent, both of them, flushed and frightened looking. Diana was pounding her gavel, trying to still the crowd. The noise died as suddenly as it had erupted, giving way to a dead, shocked silence.

My mother's face was haggard.

"We've heard the suggestion that he be killed immediately. Discussion. One at a time." Ocean raised her hand. "Yes, Ocean?"

"I remember once some of us questioned the rightness of killing animals for meat. I've heard Diana say she cannot bear to tend the goats, to watch them playing, and then participate in slaughter, even of the old and the weak. Some of us eat meat; some of us do not. Even those who do, see killing as an unfortunate necessity.

162

"The founders left a world of violence, a world, they said, where humans and animals suffered incredibly. They came here to build a better place to live. And now some of us—some of them—are saying we ought to take the life of a young and healthy human. And some of us cheer the suggestion." The room was very still. "I don't know how to answer that. But I think we have to try, calmly and meditatively, to consider alternatives that are more acceptable— more consistent, really—with our own peaceful beliefs and sensibilities." She sat again. I could see that her hands were shaking slightly. Calliope put her hand on Ocean's shoulder. Redwood rose again and was recognized.

"Ocean has been gentle and good since the day she was born. I haven't been." There was a scattering of affectionate laughter. Diana tapped her gavel once, lightly, and Redwood continued unsmiling. "I haven't been and for damned good reasons. I stand by what I've said. We might want to be peaceful and gentle, but we don't have that choice. If some of our daughters find violence hard to understand, I'm glad. Glad they've never had to live in a way that makes them want to kill." She drew a deep, uneven breath. "They've never seen a woman—a friend!—raped and dead by the side of the road. Or knifed to death because she dared to fight a man who wanted to steal her food. Or sold in the streets like an animal. You've never seen bodies floating in a river, children starving, men surviving because they were strong and knew how to fight and didn't care—" her voice broke and she sat down abruptly.

Someone was moaning softly, as though she were in mourning. Calliope's expression told me that these visions of Redwood's were new to her, too. We'd heard only vague references to violence from the elders. I looked around me at the other young women. Yes, they'd been protected from such details, too. Ocean's mouth was twisted in a grimace of pain. Angel was waving her hand at Diana, who nodded to her.

She spoke calmly and slowly. "Certainly we've seen horrors that we hope you never see. But it's now I'm concerned about. This man has brought the stupidity of his world here, to us." She looked solemnly around the room at her audience, her eyes fixing on Ocean. "This has nothing to do with what's rational or moral. The children—they know. They found out last night. Bennett isn't a playful goat. He's not a harmless fish or a rabbit or a horse. He isn't even a mountain lion, who can be frightened away with loud noises. He's not just a predator; he's the most intelligent predator of all, the one least governed by rational nature. Animals hunt for food. Men kill for power and for 'ideals.' As Redwood says, our daughters have been safe all their lives. But our granddaughters are closer to their instincts, and their instincts are true. We have to protect our homes, ourselves, and our loves. Nature kills to protect herself and to survive. She killed our civilization—no, *their* civilization—because it threatened her and her children. We need to do the same." Angel sat down amid a roar of applause, foot-stamping, whistles, and cheers, mostly from the older women.

Freedom was next to speak. "My mother has made a very good case for murder." Her voice was iced with anger. "So has Angel. But Angel forgets we're not the goddess they named this village for. And we are not nature. We're only a part of her, as Bennett is. Certainly he's hopelessly arrogant and maybe we need to be arrogant, too, in order to survive. But I don't care what happened in the past. This village is not sacred ground and killing for it is still killing." She had moved from anger to disgust. "That's all."

Luna rose and looked directly at me as she began to speak. "Redwood's right," she said as though she'd been with the founders on the way to Demeter and, unlike the rest of us, knew everything they knew. "The children were right. There's nothing to be gained by keeping the man alive unless we want to use him as an excuse." What was she driving at, I wondered. And why was she looking at me? "I know Diana doesn't think we should leave this village and start a new one as long as we have this problem to solve here." There were a few groans scattered through the room. No one wanted to hear about Luna's favorite subject, not now. I was too angry to groan, and her next words made me even angrier. "And we all know that Morgan doesn't want us to go, either, for her own reasons—"

"Shut up, Luna!" Calliope took two steps forward and shook her fist at Luna, but Luna still had the floor, and Diana ordered Calliope to be silent.

"As I was saying," Luna continued, "I can't speak for those who aren't here, but it seems to me that if Sara and Sunny were at this meeting they'd agree with me. Whatever the motive might have been for pushing this meeting while they were gone—personally, I think they're being punished —" This was too much. Several shouts of protest rose from around the room. Diana looked patient, shook her head, and tapped her gavel. Luna went on, speaking more quickly. "In any case, Bennett's presence just delays the other things we have to do, or makes people think we ought to delay them. I want him dead."

My mother nodded to me. I could feel the heat in my face as I began to speak. "I did not stop the children because I wanted Bennett alive—for *any* reason." I could barely talk through my rage. "I stopped them because I didn't want children to kill him. That's for adults to do, and to live with." I started to sit down again, but thought better of it. As long as I had the floor I might as well say my piece.

"Through no choice of my own, I seem to be constantly involved with Bennett." My head was beginning to clear and my voice relaxed somewhat. I willed my muscles to ease. I had to make my position clear. I wanted him gone, any way at all, even if the new settlement people, and Sunny, left the village for good the day after. "I understand very well, I think, what our mothers mean. They've been wrong to protect us from their experience, but I don't think they'll be able to protect us any more." I was wondering what experience Sara and Sunny would bring back to us, if they came back at all, but I wasn't going to bring that up. "As you all know," I said, trying for a bit of humor, "I'm no killer." I did get a few laughs. Everyone knew that when the time came to slaughter as much as a chicken I was nowhere around to see it. I never even went fishing. "But even though the proposal that we kill him might—only might—have come from an irrational source, I think we need to consider why it's a rational proposal." Freedom was waving her arm, waiting impatiently to be heard again. Suddenly I didn't feel like talking any more. I had said all I wanted to say.

Freedom looked at me as she began to speak, as if to apologize. "I don't like him much either, Morgan. Not any more. But I've never felt it necessary to kill everyone I don't like." She smiled slightly. I smiled back. "Maybe we don't have any choice. I honestly don't know. But I do know that if you do an evil thing to protect yourself from evil, you had better be sure, for your own sake, that the evil you're fighting is real. I don't think we know that yet. I don't even think we can begin to decide that yet. If we do, we'll be acting out of fear. I'm not ready to make a decision. Not very many of us are. We need to calm down. I won't agree to anything until we've cleared away some of this emotional underbrush." She gestured toward the group of founders who had called most loudly for his death. "How many of you," she asked, "have actually dealt with the man? He's afraid, too. He knows this meeting has to do with him, but we're not even giving him a chance to speak for himself." She stopped and looked up at Diana. "I'm not saying it well. My mother's the speaker in our family. I get tired of hearing myself talk and I have to leave for guard duty now. But my point is that we should talk about it here tonight, discuss it, shout, do anything we need to do to express our opinions, then go home and think about it some more before we make any decisions. Please." She left the room. She'd given us an out, if we wanted to take it.

Firstborn was standing, in her self-important way, and raising her hand as well. When she was given the signal to speak, she looked around the room as her mother had done before she spoke.

"My sisters," she said, smiling sweetly, "are all so eloquent. I'm almost reluctant to speak." I could not repress a loud sigh of impatience. Calliope turned around, caught my eye, and winked. "But I can't agree with Freedom. There's never any point in waiting. In fact, waiting can be dangerous. What if he escapes while we're trying to make up our minds? What if he kills someone? Our mothers have told us enough. I don't want him here." She smiled again and sat down, accompanied by light applause.

Just as Firstborn finished speaking, Athena, relieved by Freedom, returned from guard duty. She came and stood with us. Ocean, whispering, told her what the first hour had been like. When she heard what Firstborn had said, she laughed. "Always so practical."

Diana had noticed Athena entering the room. "Athena, you've just come from Bennett and Donna, haven't you? Would you like to tell us how they are?"

Athena hesitated briefly before she spoke. "I don't know that I have anything to say. He isn't talking at all. From time to time he stands up and paces the room, then throws himself down in his chair again. I stayed outside most of the time. Donna came to the window once to talk to me, to ask me about the meeting. I told her it was just a meeting, that we always have meetings, and she wasn't to worry. I had to say that. She seemed so sad." She sat down abruptly.

"Thank you," Diana said. "Have you been told where we are in this discussion?"

"Yes. I don't think I have anything to say yet," she

repeated. "I'd like to just listen for a while."

Joanna asked to be recognized. I was very much interested in hearing what she would have to say. I thought she was more truly practical than any of us, and honest.

"Like Luna . . ." she began. Oh, no, I thought. She wasn't going to quote Luna! But she had a sly look on her face. "I can't speak for those who aren't here. And I won't." I burst out laughing. Calliope grinned at me. "Besides, Sara probably wouldn't agree with me anyway." Luna's round face was flushed, her mouth set in a grim line. Joanna grew more serious. "I think there are some things that need to be said. Some things no one has mentioned. About our feelings. You've heard a lot about how angry we are, but you haven't heard the whole truth. Some of us, I think, also feel guilty—"

"No, Joanna!" Angel gasped. Diana raised her gavel but didn't bring it down again. The room was very quiet.

"Guilty about something that happened when we came here." Joanna continued. "This valley wasn't deserted when we came here—when Angel and Diana came here, first, to make sure it was safe. There was a man here. His wife and child were with him. He had a gun. He saw Diana and Angel and he started screaming at them. He said he'd kill them if they didn't leave. They dropped behind a rock and waited for him to show himself. He began to rave, saying he'd kill his wife and child if they didn't leave. They shot at him. He killed his wife and child, a tiny girl, and then he killed himself. We buried them and we didn't mark their graves. I think any of us would have done what Diana and Angel did. Any of us."

Everyone was talking at once. I looked at my mother. I had never seen her look old before. And she looked sick. The man had killed his family. She hadn't. She couldn't have known he'd actually do it. Joanna shouldn't have told. We didn't have to know. Diana hit the table hard with her gavel, only once, and the room was quiet.

"So we have anger and fear and guilt," Joanna said. "And the guilt makes us even more angry." But what about Bennett, I wanted to scream. What do you want us to do about Bennett?

"I've listened very carefully to what everyone has been saying. I couldn't help but notice that not one woman has suggested that we ought to decide, now, that we won't harm him. That we believe in the sanctity of life and will let him live. So I'll suggest it." Someone shouted "No!" and someone else yelled, "Let her speak!

She waited for the reaction to die down and continued. "This whole discussion has been negative. Either kill him now, or wait until he's done something awful, then kill him. How would any of us feel, among strangers, in a culture alien to our own, forced to work but not allowed to participate in decisions?"

"Damn it, Joanna," Redwood cried in exasperation. "Why should he get any better than we got?"

"Redwood, sit down and do not interrupt," Diana snapped, banging her gavel again. Some of the color had returned to her face. Redwood mumbled a sullen apology and took her seat. "Joanna, please continue."

"Redwood's right, of course," Joanna said. "That's exactly what it was like for us. And we wanted only to leave. Why should we expect him to be any different, any less angry? I have the same bitterness as Redwood, the bitterness we all have. I didn't want to have to start over again in a wilderness, run and hide myself away, grub for food and shelter. Now we're strong, here, in our own town, and we're behaving the way the strong, the majority, always behave. Kill him? Sure, maybe we have to. But the thought makes me sick—"

She was interrupted by a shout of "Grab him!" and sounds of a scuffle outside one of the windows. Women leaped from their benches, racing for doors and windows. I was caught in the rush to the entry doors, trapped in the middle of a crowd, unable to see what was going on.

"What is it?" someone near me called out. A woman just outside the door shouted in to us.

"It was Bennett. It's okay. We've got him now."

I got outside just in time to see two women leading him away. Freedom stood near the entry, her head in her hands, surrounded by questioners. She was saying, "I don't think he heard much."

Redwood pushed her way through to her daughter, her face dark with anger. "You did it on purpose," she accused. Freedom took her hands away from her face. A large purple bruise was beginning to swell near her temple.

"No I didn't!" She was as angry as her mother. "He hit me—not hard, but enough to stop me for a minute. I was stupid, that's all."

I spoke up. "We believe you, Freedom. Redwood—we believe her."

Angel was looking at the bruise. "She'll be all right."

Diana came to the door. "Let's get back to our meeting," she said. We all went back inside. It took some time for Diana to gavel the crowd to silence. "Does anyone else wish to speak?" The silence held. None of us looked at each other. No one raised a hand. "No? Then I'm going to end this meeting. I propose that Bennett be kept guarded in his house until we come to a decision. I propose that we meet again within the next two weeks and take a final vote on the issue. Does anyone disagree?" No hands were raised. Although it seemed clear what the decision was going to have to be, everyone was glad enough to postpone action. The meeting ended less than two hours after it had begun. No one was satisfied, except perhaps Freedom, who had wanted us to take more time to decide.

It was Joanna's argument that stayed with me. She had spoken out against killing him, yet at the same time, had agreed that we might have to. All of us were suspended, poised, waiting for something that would force us to act.

XV

Sunny and Sara returned.

We had waited with increasing fears for their safety, all but giving them up when, late one afternoon in the fourth week of their absence, they were sighted a mile out of town walking their horses down the road. They were tired and dirty, their boots worn. They'd both lost weight and had lines on their faces that hadn't been there before. But they were smiling. They had good news. They had found a site for the new village.

Athena and I were sitting at the Flower having an after-work glass of wine when someone raced past the open door shouting. All of us—there had been a dozen women at the tables around us, including Joanna—raced outside and toward the center of town, hearing only the noise, afraid of what we'd find. But then we heard laughter and cheering and we saw the reason. They stood in the middle of the road, faces flushed, eyes damp, an ecstatic circle of women dancing around them, hugging and being hugged. Joanna leapt through the crowd and hurled herself at Sara, crying loudly, almost overbalancing the smaller woman, who returned the embrace fiercely, kissing Joanna's face and neck. I thought I'd wait to welcome her. Sunny was already surrounded by new-settlement friends, and I didn't try to break through to her. She caught my eye. We smiled at each other. She looked somehow unfamiliar to me, a tall heroine, a gaunt adventurer from another world.

Luna was saying something about a "full report," but Sunny, shaking her head and walking toward me with Luna at her heels, said they were exhausted and needed sleep and food. They had done the last two days' journey to Demeter in one day, not resting, barely eating, always moving, so eager were they to return.

She put her arms around me and held me close. Over her shoulder I saw Athena, standing between Calliope and Angel, watching us blandly. Although there was nothing accusing in her look, I felt her discomfort.

"Would you like to eat first, sleep first, or what?" I said, pulling away and looking into Sunny's weary, dusty face.

"Dinner's ready in the dining hall," Luna suggested.

"Is that all right with you?" Sunny asked me. It was. I needed time to adjust to her return.

Once we got to the dining hall, the strain of Luna's presence was alleviated by the others who crowded in to sit at our table. Sara and Joanna were nowhere in sight. I didn't see Athena either. Everyone wanted to talk to Sunny at once, but they soon realized from her stumbling half-answers and concentrated eating that they would have to wait to find out more than the essentials: the scouts had found a site for the village, and it was possible to travel in the world and survive.

When she stopped eating and stopped even trying to talk, I took her home. Luna was so involved by then in discussion of the final stages of new settlement preparation that she let us get out the door alone. Sunny went directly to the bedroom and sat down on the edge of the bed. I brought a washcloth from the bathroom and wiped the dust from her face and hands. She let me help her undress, crawled under the quilt, and fell asleep. We hadn't spoken alone at all.

The next morning I let her sleep, and when I stopped by at lunch time she wasn't there. At the dining hall, I spotted her at a table with Sara, Joanna, and Luna.

"Hi, Morgan." Athena was standing next to me at the counter holding a tray of food. "Good to see them back, isn't it?" She said brightly.

"Yes. We're all very glad . . ." I began inanely. She was looking at me kindly, questioningly. I gazed back at her, feeling helpless and ambivalent.

"Well," she laughed nervously. I'd never known her to laugh nervously before. "See you tonight?" Tonight? How could I see her tonight? "At the meeting hall," she explained. "They're going to tell us about it. Sunny and Sara."

"Oh. Right. I'll see you there." I turned away from her and took my food to Sunny's table.

"There you are, Morgan." Sara stood and grasped me in a tight, bony embrace. For the first time, my relief and happiness that she was safe, that they were both safe, broke through. I kissed Sara half a dozen times, laughing and exclaiming over the skinny sight of her, here, in the dining hall with Joanna. I didn't feel self-conscious until I sat down next to Sunny, who put her arm around me. I kissed her and held her hand for a moment, smiling at everyone, including Luna.

"I've been wanting to talk to you, Morgan," Luna said, apparently encouraged by my now-regretted smile. "We're going to need your help."

"I'll talk to her about it later, Luna," Sara said.

"Might as well be now," I said, forcing another smile. Sunny and Joanna were both staring at their plates.

Sara shrugged. She looked embarrassed. "Okay. We want to take our history with us to the new settlement—the records of Demeter. Luna's collected some volunteers to help with the copying, but you're the expert. You know where everything is, and you know what can be left out if it gets to be too much."

"You're going then, Sara?"

"We both are. Joanna and I."

I avoided looking at Sunny. "I can start day after to-morrow."

"No sooner?" Luna wailed. I glared at her. At least I was going to pick my own time.

Finishing my lunch, I stood to go. "I'm really anxious to hear about your adventures tonight. You must have some incredible stories to tell."

Sara grinned and jabbed Sunny with her elbow. "We sure do!"

"Hold on, Morgan." Sunny stood up. "I'll go out with you."

We stacked our trays and walked outside.

"I hear Bennett's locked up."

Instead of going along with her attempt at small talk, I stopped and turned to her. "When are you leaving?" The muscles around my mouth were tight, the words difficult to force out.

"As soon as everything's ready and Sara and I have rested a bit. Three, maybe four weeks."

"I don't want to go with you."

"I know."

We had started walking again. She took my hand. Both of us were crying. For once I didn't care that others could see. I just wanted to walk with her and hold her hand and cry.

"Morgan? Morgan, I still want us to care about each

other. Maybe I'm making a mistake—"

"Maybe I am."

Redwood, who had been approaching us, came close enough to see our faces and veered away.

Sunny continued. "Be my friend?"

"Of course. I'm your friend." Maybe we were making a mistake, but I didn't think so. And the kind of friendship that followed being lovers took time. We didn't have much time. I began to cry harder. She tried to hold me, but the closeness confused us both. There was something so final about agreeing to be friends.

"I'll move my things out today," she said. We were walking again, but not touching.

"Where are you going?"

"Luna's got an extra room."

Suddenly angry, I turned on her. "Tell me the truth about Luna. Are you going to be lovers? Are you lovers already?"

Sunny shook her head. "I told you the truth weeks ago. No. I don't feel that way about her. Not at all. I'm only interested in what she's doing. There's no one."

That helped. It more than helped. I felt much better. I even felt sad for her.

We parted where the path turned off to the dairy. I had work to do there that afternoon. She kissed me, and we both began to cry again. Then she went back to the house to start moving her things.

The meeting hall was crowded to overflowing that night for the second time in a week. But the similarity to our last meeting ended there. Certainly, there was still some conflict about the new settlement. Some of the elders still wanted its departure delayed until the Bennett problem was disposed of one way or another. But there was no question that they were going, and whatever personal loss any of us might be suffering, all of us were involved in some way. Although I had managed to avoid helping Luna's com-

175

mittees with supply-gathering and with repair and rebuilding of wagons, even I was now to be drafted. The important decisions were made. We all had to be happy, at least, that Sara and Sunny were alive.

The two scouts were seated at the council table with Diana. When I saw Sunny up there, completely apart from me, I realized more clearly what these few weeks had done. She had changed, not just physically. The new look of maturity wasn't entirely due to the more sharply defined planes of her face. She had learned something about herself, something she had needed to know to possess herself completely.

"Morgan! Over here!" Athena was standing on a bench near the center of the room, waving at me. She had saved a seat. I had been thinking of her throughout the afternoon, trying to clarify my feelings. Nothing stood in the way of involvement now. The physical attraction was undeniable. But I was afraid. She was vulnerable and impulsive, and I couldn't be sure how much of my interest in her was based on reaction to the loss of Sunny. On one side of Athena sat Calliope and Ocean. The vacant seat was to her left and just beyond it was Donna, who tucked her feet under to let me pass. I stared at her rudely.

"Diana said I could come," she said.

Athena finished the explanation for me. Indicating the scouts with a nod, she said, "They aren't going to talk about the exact location of the new village. Angel thought it wouldn't do any harm to let her hear the rest of it. The council agreed." Still, it made me uncomfortable to have the outsider in our meeting. I might have raised a useless objection, but the woman was sitting next to me after all. I wished she were sitting somewhere else.

Luna arrived late as usual and took the fourth seat at the table in front. She pulled her chair close to Sunny's. Too close.

Sara began the story of their adventures. Sunny broke

in to remind her that they'd found an automobile and described it at length. Sara continued with her factual account, telling of their capture by the priest. Again, Sunny filled in the missing description—what he looked like, how he behaved.

Diana didn't even try to convince them to speak one at a time, but despite their repeated interruptions and corrections of each other they kept to a rough chronological order. I had been planning to rely on my memory for our records, but decided to take some notes. This deserved a full account, a part of our history that I knew would go with them to the new settlement.

Perhaps my exposure to Bennett had prepared me for the ugliness they described. In any case, I wasn't shocked by their description of the values and beliefs they had encountered. Frightened and excited, but not shocked.

Sara, in her terse, dry manner, was telling of their escape when Donna startled me by whispering in my ear. "They're very brave, aren't they?" she said and directed her attention again to the scouts before I could recover from my surprise and respond.

Sara had stopped talking and was looking at Sunny. "You tell them about the women's village," she said. The initial, joyful stir that those words created was hushed and turned to fear by the look on her face and on Sunny's, as well as by Sunny's obvious reluctance to speak.

For once, her description was bare of color and detail. She simply told us what they had found and passed on their conclusions. I expected to hear shouts of anger; there were none. I heard some soft whispers of pain around me, but my own head ached with the pressure of silent, horrified speculation. I could feel Athena gripping my arm. When I felt that I could speak I turned to Donna.

"What do you think of that," I hissed at her.

"And what do you expect?" she snapped back, loud enough for those nearby to hear. I was looking directly into her eyes, only half hearing the angry murmur of reaction just behind us. She met my look, and I saw her for the first time as a real woman instead of a symbol of something alien. Her words had been harsh, but I could see the confusion of her emotions. That's the way things were, her expression seemed to be saying, but she wasn't at all sure of how things ought to be. "Besides," she added, looking away, "Sunny said they couldn't be sure. They're only guessing."

Sara had told us about their meeting with the merchants and was describing their trek to the coast when I suddenly made a connection between what they had learned about the social structure of the man's world they had visited and the man who had been living in Demeter. He had spoken of his village.

"Bennett's a runaway, isn't he?" I whispered to Donna. She didn't answer, glancing at me out of the corners of her eyes and returning her gaze immediately to the front of the room. Of course he was. Her rigid non-reaction confirmed it. He came from a village. He belonged to a priest.

Remembering the way he had blustered into our valley, asking to see the priest, I was almost forced to admire his nerve. Trapped as he had been, he had planned to try to bluff his way through, acting indignant at this detention of a free man, hiding his fear of capture as a runaway. It occurred to me that maybe his status made him less dangerous to us. He couldn't very well go running to a priest with the news of our existence. But that pleasant thought passed quickly. All he had to do was talk, to anybody, and the talk would spread to those with power. The problem was the same.

Sunny was describing the beach, and Ocean was listening raptly. She'd never seen the water she'd been named for, and eyes closed, she was trying to see it in Sunny's words. Calliope looked sad and thoughtful, as if her mind were on something else. She didn't come out of her reverie until Sara, making us all laugh, told of her dreamy attempt to turn on the television they'd found in the abandoned mill town. It was the town itself that captured my interest. A remnant of the industrial past. No more lumbering. No more mills. No more town, its houses and its businesses disappearing piece by piece until there'd be nothing left for the scavengers to take. I thought about the fishing village and wondered how their seagoing boats were different from our little lake vessel, the fishing boat Sara called a "rowboat with a sail."

Their travels back to Demeter had been less eventful, or at least less thrilling. They had passed within sight of another priest's village, but their claim to be extra sons was accepted, and they allowed themselves to be hurried along the road by the priest's soldiers. For a few miles they followed an old railroad track. The torn-up roadbed led them to a rusty freight car, sitting like an island, useless broken track on either side. A man and a child, seeing them coming, fled inside the box car, sliding the door after them and shouting incoherently.

Most important, they found what they were looking for: a green valley cut by a clean small river that promised fish and water for crops. The surrounding hills were well-wooded. They estimated that the land was about a hundred fifty miles southwest of Demeter, and that there were no settlements of any kind within forty miles. To be sure of its isolation, they had spent a full week exploring the land beyond and around it. They believed it was fertile and safe. They had carefully mapped the route from the new valley to Demeter with sheet after sheet of detailed notations and little drawings of landmarks.

Sunny looked tired, as though the recitation of their journey had wiped away her night's rest. She sank back in her chair while Sara, concluding the narrative, asked if anyone had any questions.

Luna raised her hand, her head tilted to one side, her expression, for once, uncertain. She wanted to know more about the site they had found for the new village.

"There's nothing there? No buildings? Nothing to start with?"

Sunny shook her head. "Nothing. But there are trees and water, the weather's good, the location is sheltered. It's perfect. Of all the possible sites, it was by far the best. We should be able to put together some rough shelters to see us through the first winter."

"Yes," Luna said. "I suppose we could." She didn't sound particularly happy. Sara was laughing.

XVI

Athena and I had made plans to ride out past the northern hill and spend the day at the lake. The mornings were still cool, but when I stepped outside my door, carrying my lunch in a cloth bag, the early sunlight felt warmer than it had. A little nervous and anxious about the day's prospects, I stood on my doorstep trying to make up my mind. Would a lighter sweater than the one I wore be more comfortable? But if I stopped now to change, I might possibly be late. Finally, laughing at myself, I rushed back in the door, changed, and rushed out again.

Athena was there waiting at the stables when I arrived. She looked casual and at her ease. I didn't believe she was. We had not been alone together since she had visited my house during the first week of Sunny's absence. For the past week, since Sunny and I had made our separation formal, Athena and I had been circling around each other tensely.

She had already led two of the smaller mares out of their stalls and had fitted them with bridles. Our bags strapped to our shoulders, we mounted in the stable yard. Only once, when I was very young, had I vaulted to the back of a horse. Angel had caught me doing it. She had pulled me down again, slapped me hard across the back, and said, "How do you like the way that feels?" She had then sent me to the fields to work.

We skirted the playing field and rode slowly through the lane that led to the path over the hill. To our left, the winter wheat, tall but still green, rippled softly in the breeze. Although most of the other fields had been plowed and planted early in the spring, we passed a group of a dozen women, near the upslope, seeding the fresh-plowed earth with hot-weather crops. They greeted us as we rode by them and began our climb.

It felt good to have the warm back of a horse under me, to feel its muscles rippling as it walked the path, moving surely among the small rocks that dotted the hillside.

By the time we reached the ridge and saw the lake below us, the sun was halfway to noon, and even my light sweater was feeling warm. We stopped while I took it off and tied its arms around my waist. Athena had worn only a shirt and shorts. I glanced down at the village. I was glad to leave it for a day, to try to forget about the departure of the new settlement, now only two weeks away, and about our continuing division over Bennett. The second meeting was to be held in three days, after Calliope's Demeter ceremony, and despite a lot of proselytizing on both sides, no one had budged from her original position.

I felt weighed down by my own anxiety and by our lack of decision. Why was it so hard? Too many things were hard. Simple things, like loving and not having, fearing and not being able to kill. It occurred to me that maybe things were harder, in the end, for those who had it easy most of the time. The confusion was greater. There was more time, more space than there ought to be, and that allowed pain to grow bigger than it needed to be. Was that possible? Athena was looking at me, waiting for me to stop dreaming and begin the descent to the lake.

"Sorry," I said, smiling. I told her my thoughts as we started down.

"Harder? For those who have it easy?" She shook her head, laughing. "I don't see how that could be, Morgan. Not really, anyway. But I think I understand what you mean. Look what you're doing right now—fretting and philosophizing, making things complicated when they're not complicated at all."

"Things are complicated."

"Only when there's time for them to be."

I grunted, beginning to resent what seemed to me to be a superior attitude.

She flushed. "You're right. That sounded smug. But it's true. When you have to make a decision, you make it. Especially if it's a life-and-death issue. Our mothers and grandmothers remember the real battles. They remember well enough to know what action they want to take without endless mumbling and worrying. I don't think Sunny is having much trouble with it, not after what she's seen."

I was startled. "But you don't want to kill him, do you? I didn't think you did."

"I don't want to *have* to kill him. There's a difference. We don't have a choice."

On the shore near the foot of the path, a fishing party was hauling a net, silver and frantic with dying fish, from the boat to the gravelly beach. Without stopping to greet them, I turned to the right. They were intent on their work, and it was work that never had appealed to me. "Nice catch," Athena said. "We're having good fishing this spring." I nodded, gazing at the glittering lake, letting the mare find her own way over the shoreline rubble. The water was high and clearer than it had been in other years.

183

The lake was fed by a meandering stream that came down from the mountains to the northeast—where there had been heavy snow that winter—circled the southern side of the valley, and flowed west into the lake's basin.

I touched my horse's flanks with my heels, urging it to a gallop, and sped off, feeling a lightness and a sense of freedom that I hadn't felt for a long time. I wanted to move fast. I heard Athena right behind me, then saw her alongside. We raced for a hundred yards before we slowed again to a walk. The day was beautiful, the lake was beautiful, and there was no reason to dwell on anything else.

As if she were reading my mind, Athena said, "Let's forget about it all for today, all right? There is no Bennett. There is no new settlement. There is no Demeter. We don't know those fisherwomen. We don't live anywhere and we're stopping by the side of this lake on our way to nowhere."

"Very poetic," I laughed. "That just makes me feel lost."

We dismounted near an outcropping of rocks and scrub oaks and looped the horses' reins around the scraggly branches. The breeze felt chilly in the shade, and we moved quickly out into the sun again and close to the water. Athena began immediately to remove her clothing.

"I'm going in. Want to join me?"

I shook my head. "Not yet. I want to warm up a bit first." I watched her walk down to the water and step carefully in. I heard her gasp. "Cold?" I said.

"Very." She smiled back at me. "But I'll adjust." She stood in water just above her knees for a moment, waiting for her body to accept the coldness. She was still white from the winter past, but her paleness had a golden cast to it. Suddenly, she rushed in up to her waist and dove. She came up breathing hard. "Cold!" she shrieked. "Come on in. It feels great."

"You're freezing! Why should I be as crazy as you

are?" But I began to undress. The cold water and the exercise were just what I needed, although normally I preferred swimming in July and August when the water had warmed. I walked to the edge. I'd show her, I thought. I didn't hesitate, but ran right in, splashing lustily. It was cold! It stopped my breath. I swam out to her.

"Feels better already, doesn't it?"

"No. It's frigid. If it were any colder it wouldn't be liquid at all." I dove down to the bottom, skimming the sand, looking around me at the weeds and the fish. Sometimes, you could find fossils from the time when the ocean had come this far inland. I hunted as long as my breath held and settled this time for a smooth red stone. I surfaced with it in my mouth and held it out on my tongue for Athena to see. We treaded water, close together, while she examined it.

"Give it to me," she said, her eyes teasing. I had started the game, and she was going to make me finish it. She opened her mouth. The challenge was irresistible. I passed the stone from my tongue to hers. She held it as if she were tasting it, then passed it back to me again. Our lips together, forgetting myself, I began to sink, giving us both a noseful of water. Blowing and coughing, I lost the stone and opened my eyes to see her feet sliding below the water. I followed her down.

She was searching the bottom. I swam around her, behind her, watching her as she searched. My lungs did not hold as long as hers, and I rose to the top and waited for her. She came up soon after.

"I couldn't find it," she said, "but I brought you another one."

It was green with veins of red. She held it in her palm, to show me, then popped it in her mouth and swam for shore.

Again I found myself following her. I stumbled up on the beach, shivering with cold, feeling even more tense and slightly embarrassed at my impulsive game with the first stone. She was gathering our clothes, carrying them to a patch of grass unshaded by rocks or scrub. She spread them out for us to sit on.

"I'm hungry," she said, walking to where the horses were tethered, returning with the bags of cheese, bread, and dried fruit that we both had brought. I was hungry too, and delighted to see her pull a small corked jug from her bag.

"Wine." She waved it at me. "It will warm us up."

"Wonderful idea," I said with real appreciation. She held it out for me to take the first swallow. It was good wine, from one of our rare vintage years. She took the jug from me and drank, then corked it and set it between us. We sat close together eating slowly, looking at the lake. The women across the way were filling their baskets with fish, folding their net, preparing to take their loaded wagon back over the hill to the village.

After our meal, we lay back in the sun, now turning hot, our muscles relaxing in the warmth. I allowed myself to feel the heat, to smell the lake, and began to drift completely in my senses, nearly mindless. But I was aware of Athena beside me, close. Her hand brushed mine, then caught and held tightly.

"If we fall asleep," I said to break our silence, "will you burn? Your skin is still so white."

"Maybe just a little. But I never burn badly. I turn yellow."

"Gold, you mean?" I said seriously. She opened her eyes and turned to look at me.

"Let's. Let's sleep for a while." I didn't think I would be able to, but I did.

When we woke, the sun was still high and hot. It had moved only an hour's distance across the sky. I woke first. Our hands were still touching, and when I stirred, Athena woke too. She moved closer to me, and I cradled her head on my shoulder. Her hair smelled like sunlight. She smelled warm. I noticed a slight reddening of the skin on her shoulder.

"You have burned, a little."

"So have you, right across here." She touched my cheek, running her finger lightly across my nose to the other side of my face.

"Maybe we should get dressed." I didn't really want to.

"Not yet. The sun feels so good. What's wrong with your neck?"

Unconsciously, with my free hand, I'd been rubbing the side of my neck. "Nothing. It's just a little stiff. I must have slept wrong."

"Even after swimming? You must have a lot of tension in your body. This has been a hard time for you." She sat up. "Roll over on your stomach. I'll rub your back."

I turned over awkwardly. The grass tickled my nose and left me suspended in a sneeze that never quite came, that almost came but went away again when I felt her hands on my neck, kneading, searching gently for the knotted places. I felt her fingers probe the base of my skull and move down the sides of my neck to my rigid shoulders.

"I'm afraid you're going to have a hard time making me relax."

"I expect you to help. Loosen up. Feel the sun. Feel my hands. And don't think!"

I laughed. She seemed to know my weaknesses very well.

She worked the muscles lightly at first, then more firmly as they began to loosen. I turned my face toward the water, smooth and blue, stretching for a mile to the far shore, and sighed.

"That's good." She slid her hands down to the middle of my back, kneading, touching, rubbing, running her palms along my sides to my waist. "Turn your head the other way for a while now." I did, and she rubbed my neck again as I watched the horses nibbling at the wild oats sprouting between the rocks. She moved her body down along my side until I could no longer feel her above me and began to massage my feet, taking first one, then the other, finding the places where there was pain and rubbing it away.

The ache in my neck and shoulders began to subside. I was almost sorry when I felt her hands leave my feet and move up my calves, kneading deeply, until I felt her move higher, to my thighs. I suppressed a groan, not ready to give in yet to my feelings, but she knew. When she reached the tops of my thighs she stopped, breathed deeply, and leaned again over my back, returning to my shoulders while I could still feel her touch on my legs. Her hands slid down along my shoulder blades, and she touched the sides of my breasts as she stroked me. She was sweating slightly. I could smell it. So was I. My skin became so sensitive that a small wrinkle in the clothing beneath me became unbearably irritating.

"I have to . . ." I said, gesturing vaguely. She sat back while I smoothed the shirt that had covered the soft ground under my breasts, then thought better of it and lifted the shirt away. She kissed my shoulder. I hesitated, looking at her, but she smiled and, with a movement of her arm, invited me to lie down again on my stomach. I did, and again felt her hands on my back, along my sides, moving down to my hips and below them.

"I like the shape of your bottom," she said, and I could hear the smile in her voice as she massaged first one side, then the other, in large, circular movements, lifting my hips, pressing me against the ground, making my hips move in her hands. I could feel my own warm dampness. Then she was astride me, her thighs brushing mine. Beginning to feel impatient, I moved slightly as if to turn on my back, but she held me there, teasing, still kneading in that circular way, heating my skin with the friction of her hands.

188

My hips moved, and continued to move, although she was now stroking my sides. I felt her reach down, between my legs, and touch me briefly for the first time. Then she pulled back again.

"Athena . . ." She kissed the small of my back. "I want to touch you." She laughed softly and lay down full length on my back, kissing my neck, pressing against me. "Athena —" She rolled off me.

I turned over onto my back. She lay at my side. We kissed lightly and held each other, pressing tightly, deeply into each other, my thigh between hers, hers between mine, moving against each other, kissing more deeply, as if we were exchanging breath. We moved together, kissing, stroking each other's back, warm in the sun, smelling the crushed grass, her fingers in my hair, her wetness on my leg and mine on hers. I pulled away slightly and pressed her gently down on her back, stroking her breasts, kissing them, holding the nipple between my lips, feeling its hardness in my mouth. She reached to touch me and held my breast cupped in her hand while she stroked my belly, running her fingers down through my pubic hair. I gasped as she touched me and reached for her. She turned, pushing my shoulders down, not so gently, until I lay on my back again. We laughed and kissed, and she made love to me softly, surely, until I cried out and lay limp—for a moment only, because I wanted her.

I turned on my side and bit her shoulder, sucking at it, running my hand down across her breasts, down across her stomach, touching her, sliding my fingers into her. She groaned and breathed shallow and fast, and I stroked her until with a whimpering sigh she subsided and smiled, one tear in the corner of her eye.

XVII

"What kind of ceremony can you possibly have in the middle of the woods?" Firstborn, among the first to arrive at the clearing, had been walking about, looking at the food on the table, lifting every cover, expressing disappointment at each new discovery.

"At my Demeter feast, everybody could see everything that was going on. It was a dignified, adult ceremony, right out there on the playing field."

Calliope laughed. She said nothing, probably because Athena was there with us, but I thought I knew what she was thinking. We had both had the same reaction to Firstborn's Demeter performance. Calliope had departed on that day from her usual easy acceptance of other women's quirks. We had been standing together watching, as Firstborn marched around the playing field holding her cup of ceremonial tea, leading an appointed procession of self-conscious and embarrassed women in a full circle before she stopped, raised the cup, and drank. "There she goes," Calliope had said, loudly enough for several women nearby to hear. "Now she's going to say 'cock-a-doodle-doo.' "

Firstborn continued her survey of Calliope's feast, banging the last lid down on its plate with dramatic finality. "And there's no meat!"

"I don't eat it, you know," Calliope replied.

"Well, I do."

"Well, it's my picnic."

Athena and I left them pouting at each other like children and went to join my mother, who had, with the help of Angel, Redwood, and Joanna, carried the big, clumsy picnic table to the center of the clearing. She was building a small cooking fire "for the tea," she said.

"You're making Calliope's tea?"

"Yes. She asked me to make it and present it to her, in place of her mother." It was an old tradition in the village that a woman's mother participate in the ceremony or that, if her mother was dead, as in Calliope's case, another elder be chosen.

"That's very nice," I said, knowing Diana was pleased that Calliope had selected her.

She nodded, smiling. But in the time it took to hang the kettle over the fire, her face grew serious. "I wish the good will were more general." She glanced toward Luna and some of her younger new-settlement friends, standing together at the edge of the clearing.

Athena shrugged. "There's not much anyone can do about that. Besides, it's just Luna and some of her earliest converts. They can't accept acceptance."

I laughed affectionately, appreciating her analysis. "That's right. Luna's whole personality is geared to rebellion."

"Well, she's won, or her cause has," my mother said,

still unsmiling. "And they still act as if their new settlement has nothing to do with the rest of us. They won't listen to anyone who's not going."

I looked at her quizzically. I didn't point out that she was still referring to "their" settlement. Most of us had accepted it as ours. Apparently my mother was still having trouble letting go.

She caught my look and responded defensively. "Surely, Morgan, you don't think now is a good time to go? There's still too much disagreement about Bennett. I don't think we're going to be able to make a decision this week, either. Then what?"

"Then they'll go anyway." I spoke harshly, and Athena caught my eye, soothing the pain.

Sara had come to stand near us. My mother turned to include her in the conversation. "You agree with me. That it would be better to wait. That you shouldn't leave with this Bennett thing hanging over our heads."

Sara pursed her lips and looked judicious, nodding slowly. Then she surprised us all by saying "Forget it." Diana stared at her old friend in disbelief.

"How can you say that? We've dredged up all the bad memories. We're arguing among ourselves. Freedom asked me where we buried that family, those three people who died here. She wants to put up a marker! How can you leave until we've had the chance to come together again?"

"Diana, nobody's coming apart. It's not a good time, but it's time anyway." Sara looked hard at my mother. "I know you want Demeter to be perfect and perfectly peaceful, but it's not going to happen even if you keep everybody here until the next doomsday working at it. Accept it. Let it go."

My mother was stubborn. "But we'll be losing thirty of our best women. Now, of all times. I'm not actively opposing you. I'm just asking you to listen to reason."

"It's not a matter of active opposition," Sara said more

gently. "It's a matter of attitude. We're not betraying you, Diana."

I could see that my mother was shaken. She was looking deeply into her friend's eyes, as though she were looking there for her own motives. I felt that Sara was being unfair. Diana's investment in Demeter was so complete that it really *was* her work of art. And some of her apprentices were leaving before it was finished.

I didn't like seeing my mother on the defensive. "What about their attitude?" I interjected, indicating with a jerk of my head Luna's elite corps.

Sara looked directly at me. "Their attitude has to do with something you've never felt and Diana's forgotten." I nearly cringed at the sharpness in her voice. Diana just looked puzzled. So did Athena. "Damn it, Diana, don't you remember? It used to be a normal part of adolescence—hostility toward those you love, hostility that exists so you can break away. It happens in small ways here all the time." I was insulted. I had felt it, no matter what Sara said. Didn't she remember? When we were seven years old, Calliope and I had run away and managed to walk three miles before Angel came and dragged us back to the valley. "Now it's happening in a bigger way. Maybe all the motives aren't so noble, but the goal itself is."

"They're grown women!" I said indignantly.

"No," Sara said, casting a wry glance in Luna's direction. "They're not. You don't grow up in your mother's lap. But some of us are grown, and that will be enough." She put her hand on my mother's shoulder and gazed at her intently. "Diana, they're scared. They're about to leave everything they know and care about. They have to convince themselves that they don't care." She dropped her hand. "I'm going to go get some food. See you later." Sara walked away toward the picnic table, where a large and hungry crowd was beginning to gather.

"Luna's still obnoxious," Athena said loyally.

Diana only looked at us. Then, turning away, she asked quietly, "Morgan, do you think I'm getting old? In my mind, I mean?"

"No. I don't think you're any more rigid in your thinking than I am."

We laughed together. "Is that good?" she wanted to know.

I took Athena's arm and my mother's. "Let's eat. Let's celebrate Calliope's soon-to-be daughter. Let's not worry about our minds." We walked to the near end of the table, where Calliope and Luna were talking. Luna was leaning toward Calliope, who stood straight, half turned away. She was telling Calliope that her baby should be born in the new settlement. My mother drifted away to talk to some of her friends. I, too, would have circumnavigated the conversation, but Calliope drew me into it.

"What do you think of that, Morgan?"

"Of what exactly?" I knew she was enlisting my support in her argument, but I was reluctant.

Luna spoke before Calliope had a chance to. "I was telling Calliope that her child should have the chance to grow up in a vital new town."

"And I was telling Luna that my child will like it here. And if she doesn't, she can start her own new settlement. I'm not interested in risking her unborn life in that wasteland out there, no matter what Luna says."

But Luna wouldn't let it go. "There are enough people here already. More than enough. Adding one more woman to the population won't accomplish anything."

Calliope flushed and took a step toward Luna, who backed away. "I'm not trying to accomplish anything. I'm just a cowardly dolt, and I don't like being proselytized. Ocean and I want to stay. We're going to stay."

I didn't know whether Luna was smart enough to drop the subject even then, and although I wouldn't have minded seeing Calliope hit her, I interceded. "Luna, can't we just have a nice, peaceful celebration—"

She turned on me. "Doesn't anything ever shake you loose, Morgan?"

I felt myself grow cold. I glared at her. "Yes. Some things do. I wish you'd all go away and get it over with." My fists were clenched at my sides.

She glared back at me. I think she was actually considering saying something more. But she turned suddenly and walked away.

The social groups that day sifted down into a triangular arrangement. At the apex, gathered appropriately at the end of the clearing nearest the road, was Luna's group. They projected an air of swashbuckling adventure edged with arrogance. At the second point of the triangle, under a neutral stand of trees, were those of us who planned to stay in Demeter, wished the new settlement well, and didn't feel like arguing about when they should or should not go. There were younger women and elders in our group. At the third point were those who still felt conflict over the new settlement or who criticized them for refusing to delay their departure. Redwood was the core of this group, which included many women, young and old, who felt that there were two issues that far outweighed the importance of the new settlement: Bennett, and the women living in captivity somewhere to the west whose village—a sister village to ours—had been destroyed. They stood or sat in clusters nearest the table, talking about the next day's "Bennett meeting" and concentrated weapons training.

None of the groups stayed completely to itself. Joanna and Sara moved freely, talking to everyone. Diana and Angel spent some time with us, as we did with them. Angel was wearing her new hat, a very good copy of the original. I took care to compliment Athena on her work. Her grandmother was very proud of it. Redwood, like Joanna and Sara, moved from group to group. Luna and Sunny made a brief foray into our neutral corner, but Sunny was uncomfortable with Athena and couldn't quite look at us, together, directly. Most of the women there that day were there for the party, and although they thought the new settlement, Redwood's campaign for military action, and the problem of Bennett were all very exciting, they had no particular allegiances and wandered wherever impulse took them, unaware or uncaring that our three-point formation represented anything more than conversational accident. The children divided their time between the table and the woods. Donna, of course, could not be allowed at the ceremony and was under guard with Bennett.

About two hours into the picnic, after everyone had more or less overeaten and felt the need to walk around a bit, Luna, Diana, Angel, and Joanna all found their way to our stand of trees at the same time. Athena and I were talking to Diana when we heard Joanna say loudly, "You can't be serious, Luna."

"And why not?" Luna sounded belligerent enough to attract our attention more fully.

When Joanna beckoned to my mother, saying, "Diana, you have to hear this," we moved reluctantly closer to the combatants.

"Hear what?"

"She thinks elders should be banned from the new-settlement council for the first five years." Joanna's attitude was sardonic, but her anger and disbelief showed.

"I don't want to talk about it really," Diana said. "You'll have to settle it among yourselves." She began to walk away.

Luna stopped her. "Don't go, Diana. I think we ought to have this out."

"Have what out? I have no argument with you, Luna."

"That's not true. You want us to stay." Her stance was belligerent. She was still the challenger. Sunny, who had been standing near the table, looked up at the sound of Luna's voice and strolled over to join us.

"No. I think there should be a new settlement. I don't like the idea of it happening right now, but things happen when they happen." Diana was talking to Luna, but she was looking at Joanna with great love: if Joanna and Sara wanted it, Diana did.

Luna looked disappointed. Then she smiled. "You're just saying that because you know we're going to do it and you feel you have to give your approval. Well, I don't care about your approval. This may be your village, an elders' village, but ours won't be." Her eyes narrowed. "You're not my matriarch."

Sunny reacted angrily. "Luna! There's no justification for that." Diana, her face expressionless, was silent, looking fully at Luna for the first time.

Angel stepped forward. "Perhaps," she said coolly, "you want to be matriarch of your own village."

"There's no need for that, either, Angel," Diana said, recovering. "I think it's time for the ceremony." She left the tense circle and went to the cooking fire to brew the tea. Calliope, pulling from her pocket the flower she had chosen, went with her.

Sunny was scowling at Luna. "That was a rotten thing to say. I care about Diana and about what she thinks. You're not in charge of this expedition, and I don't want anyone to think you're speaking for the rest of us."

Luna shrugged. "I guess I got a little carried away. But I had to say what I was thinking."

"Did you?" Athena snapped at her.

"And what you say or even think about our age is irrelevant too," Joanna said. "We're going. And so are some of the other old fools. And you're not going to have everything your way. We can settle our age differences some other time. That's not what we're here for today."

Diana was carrying the little pot of tea made of the dried flower of the Demeter plant, carrying it carefully to the table. Calliope held a cup. Women and girls were gathering around the table, coming together from their places in the clearing and the woods, gathering, as far as was possible, within sight of the ceremony that was about to begin. Athena and I moved in as close as we could, our arms around each other.

Calliope had decided to make the celebration a little more elaborate than she'd originally planned. She wanted to include a tribute to Aunt Helen, who had discovered the properties of the flower she had named Demeter, after the goddess of fertility, of harvest, and of avenging motherhood. It was a story we had all grown up with, the legend of an old woman who had made what was, to her, a terrifying discovery. Until she had given the seeds to Angel, she had told no one. And if the reason for their parthenogenetic pregnancies occurred to any of Aunt Helen's neighbors, they didn't say anything either, probably for fear of being thought insane. She had told Angel that she believed other herbalists had made the same discovery and kept the same secret.

For all we knew, they had. But our mothers had not believed the story until Angel, well settled in the new village, had tried it out. Although many women still didn't believe that the flower alone was the cause, no one had yet been able to conceive without it.

Now Diana was pouring the tea into Calliope's cup. Calliope raised the cup, and everyone was silent. Athena was holding my hand.

"To the memory of Aunt Helen," she said, "who knew when to keep a good thing to herself." She raised her free hand to silence the laughter and applause. "Wait, I'm not finished—and who was wise enough to pass the knowledge on to someone who would use it well." She emptied her cup to the accompaniment of cheers, and the ceremony was over.

Sunny left to relieve Bennett's guard, and Luna left with her. We entered the disintegration stage of the picnic, women moving aimlessly about the clearing. The climax had passed, but not wanting the holiday to end, some of us were making plans to carry on the celebration on our own. I was helping Calliope to clear the last of the food and mess from the table when we heard Luna shouting.

"He's gone! He's run away!" She raced to the center of the clearing. A young woman ran to her, fearfully, asking about the guard. "She's hurt, but she'll live." Angel ran out of the clearing, on her way to see what she could do for the injured woman.

"And Sunny?" I wailed, gripping Luna's shoulders as racing, pushing women ran past us out of the woods.

"She went after him."

XVIII

    I turned and ran from the clearing, Athena close behind me. The roadway, all of the village that I could see, looked like the photographs in the old newspaper. People running. Weapons. Anger and fear and shouting. A riot. A scattered army of individuals on horseback and on foot, of small bands of women running together, armed with hoes, shovels, knives, clubs, bows—whatever they could find. I followed along. The movement was toward the eastern hill, where the woman and man had first appeared. Some of the women turned off the road, headed for the stables. Athena and I turned that way too, until Redwood, on horseback and brandishing a butcher knife, reined her horse to a stop across the path, waving us back to the main road.

    "There are no more horses," she said. "Go on foot. He's up there." She pointed at the hill and galloped off. We turned, not thinking, following her direction. All of us, going to the hill, women and children. It didn't occur to me then to wonder why we were all going, and I didn't wonder what we would do when we got there, wherever "there" was. We were going to stop him, that was all.

A hand grabbed my shoulder, breaking the rhythm of my movement. I spun, impatient, not wanting to be slowed, and faced Donna. She was crying, looking around her in a panic. I tried to pull away, but she held my arm tightly.

She was sobbing. "Stop them, Morgan." Her words were barely intelligible. "They're going to kill him."

I didn't react to what she said. Her tears, her pathetic face only enraged me. I had lost sight of Athena. Everyone was going without me. "Let go of me!" I roared at her. "We've got to catch him."

"Please!" She was striking at my arms and face with her fists. I grabbed them. "Make your mother stop them. You won't catch him. He's gone. He was halfway over the hill when Sunny saw him. You won't catch him!"

"He left you here," I said deliberately.

"He's coming back. He said he would. To rescue me."

I doubted it. I pulled away, dropping her hands. I could see groups of women already starting up the hill and some circling its base to the other side. The hillside was partly wooded, but there were bare and rocky patches where a man would be clearly visible from this end of town. I didn't see him, only the women.

"Morgan! Hop on!" It was Sara, driving two horses and a wagon carrying a half dozen women including Angel and Firstborn. She slowed the wagon. I jumped for the tailgate and Angel pulled me up.

"Sunny went after him," I said. But they all knew that, and I'm not sure anyone heard me in the clatter of the wagon and the confusion of the great, choking clouds of dust it raised. I noticed that Angel was holding the rifle she had brought to the valley. I had watched her practicing with it once, and I knew she was a fair shot, but although she kept it always in the house, she never talked about it. I brought my lips close to her ear and shouted over the noise, "Where's Diana?"

"Around the other way. She's got a horse."

"How's the guard?" She nodded in reply. The guard was all right.

At the base of the hill, the stream of women spread out, some going up the road, some running or riding around to either side, as if by a planned and directed strategy. All our attention was directed at that hill, all, that is, but Angel's attention. She was looking behind us toward the west, a worried expression on her face. I followed her gaze and understood. She was looking at the sun, low in the sky. We had perhaps an hour of daylight left, an hour before the advantage would be with the solitary fugitive. There were a thousand places in this country where darkness would hide him.

Sara took our wagon up the road. About halfway up, the going got steep. Three of us jumped out to lighten the load for the horses, running, trying to keep up with the wagon. When she reached the crest, Sara stopped to wait for us. "Keep going!" Firstborn shouted, banging her hoe on the side of the wagon. Sara ignored her.

We climbed on again, and Sara released the brake and shouted the horses to a gallop down the slope. On the shallow plain below, in the long shadow of our hill, the women were converging on a small oak wood, no more than a large stand of trees, that lay to the right of the road beyond the stream. We would have to cross that stream, as others were doing now, dozens of them, a steady swell of them, led by those on horseback, surrounding the oaks, disappearing among the trees.

At the foot of the hill, Sara pulled the reins and we turned sharply to the right at a dead run, the wagon nearly tipping us all out onto the hard-packed clay beside the stream. We forded it with a series of drenching lunges and rolled up onto the other side. She had to drive more carefully now; our friends were all around us, and our slower movement made it possible for us to hear the shouts and make sense of them. He was in the wood, they said, or they thought he was, or someone had said he was.

The distance between the stream and the woods was no more than a hundred yards, rough ground with not even a track for the wagon. We had not gone even a fifth of the way when Sara, intent on the woods, gave it up.

"Everybody out," she shouted, but we were out and running before she'd finished saying it. I took a few steps, clumsy after the jarring ride, fell to my knees, and pushed myself upright with one motion. Angel was ahead of me, holding her rifle lightly in her hand. We reached the woods running hard, too hard for the tangled undergrowth and close-growing trees. I could feel the women around me, and I could see them and hear their movement and the crackling of twigs and the skittering of stones they kicked, but in the dimness of the woods there was no shouting, not even curses or cries of frustration at the obstacles to our passage. We didn't know where Bennett was. He could be anywhere in the woods. But each of us felt that the woman ahead of her knew.

We would have done better to have gone around the trees to the other side. We had passed nearly all the way through, gasping, bleeding from our scratches, when we found him, his back against a tree at the edge of the stand, a circle of horsewomen around him in the sparseness of the last few trees. Others who had come on foot ahead of us stood panting, their weapons hanging from limp arms. I pushed my way through, looking for Sunny, and found her just inside the circle, motionless, watching, a shovel in her hand. I heard Athena, suddenly at my side, say "She's all right, Morgan." I reached blindly for her hand, unwilling to take my eyes from the sight of Bennett, remembering when I had seen him surrounded this way before, with the children. But now he was breathing in deep sobs, his clothes torn, his face and arms scraped and bleeding, his lips drawn back in a snarl. He crouched, holding a large club, a tree branch, swinging it every time a woman approached him. Over and over again, a woman would approach, he would lunge, and she would back away again and watch while another woman took the same tentative steps. I saw Calliope across the circle with a bow in her hands. Redwood, holding the big knife, dismounted and began to move slowly toward Bennett, carefully, measuring his stance and the swing of his club. There was nothing tentative about her. His wild eyes settled on her and focused, less crazed than afraid.

"Mother!" It was Freedom, breaking the tension of quiet, the rhythm of watchfulness. She ran from the crowd and stood half in front of, half beside Redwood, who turned reluctantly to meet her daughter's eyes. The two women looked deeply at each other, while Bennett, his club-wielding arm jerking in spasms of readiness, watched them, his eyes flickering from one to the other. A shaft of late sun shone gold on his shoulder.

Redwood's arm dropped to her side. She and Freedom moved together back out of the circle, brushing past Calliope still rigidly poised with her bow.

Diana, sitting straight and somber on a tall bay, not ten feet from Bennett, began to talk softly and rapidly to him. "Drop it. Just drop the club and come toward me. It's all right. Just drop it and come toward me." He glanced at her, faltering, wiping the sweat from his eyes, and then at Angel, who stood beside my mother's horse, the rifle up and aimed at his head. He gripped his club more tightly, trying to watch all the women at once, crouching, swaying from side to side, his body rocking rhythmically in small parodies of lunges.

"If we all go for him at once, he can't fight us," Sara said loudly.

"No, Sara." Joanna stepped carefully into the circle. "Come on, Bennett. Drop it." She carried no weapon, but advanced on him. He stood still, staring at her. I thought he might give up. His face held no expression that I could read. And then he began to rock again, and when she came within range he struck out with his club, barely missing her head. She jumped back.

"Just drop it. Drop it and come toward me." My mother resumed her soft litany, saying the words over and over again. But they didn't reach him. He struck out fiercely at anyone who took so much as a step into the circle.

"Give it up, Bennett!" I recognized Luna's voice from the watching crowd, although I could not see her.

His mouth formed the word "no," although he made no sound. He stooped suddenly and with his free hand picked a rock from the ground. He hurled it into the crowd, in the direction of Luna's shout. It grazed a mare, which shrieked and reared and nearly threw its rider. Angel raised her rifle and again aimed it at his head; she looked as though she were about to shoot. Joanna picked up a large, flat rock and advanced a few steps, her face hard now. There was no sound but the wordless crooning of the rider to her injured mare, a soothing, calming sound in the background of a scene of tension about to break.

It was then that Sunny walked into the clearing, holding her shovel in both hands. Diana reached down from her mount and touched Angel's hair. Startled, Angel jerked her head up, saw Sunny, and hesitated, her finger still on the trigger. Joanna stopped where she was. I heard someone near me sigh. It was Jana, watching, hypnotized. Angel nodded to Diana. Joanna began to back out of the clearing, the rock still in her hand. The injured mare and its rider were silent.

Suddenly, the women around me had become spectators. They had let go of the decision and the act and had given them to Sunny. She would do it. They were just watching, and what they were watching was not quite real. If it had not been Sunny in the clearing, if it had been anyone but Sunny, or Athena, or perhaps Calliope, I could have withdrawn too. But part of me was inside of Sunny, and for that part, this was real.

I could see by the way Sunny moved, the way she held her head, that all her energy and concentration were bent on the man. She had followed him, she had raced after him, ahead of the horsewomen. She had found him and had been afraid that he would escape from her before the others would come.

The patches of golden sunlight were gone. Bennett's bare chest, his face, were gray in the twilight, glazed with sweat. He shivered. I felt an instant's pity, but no more than that. He would kill her if he could. Athena was beside me. We didn't touch.

Sunny stood within five feet of him, holding the shovel horizontally across her body. She took a half step in, and he swung at her, missed, and swung again. She brought her shovel up into the second swing, almost knocking the club from his hands. He strengthened his grip and, howling, charged her. The charge seemed to take a long time, and then his club was whistling past her shoulder, down toward it and past it as she stepped outside the blow and, in the same motion, brought her shovel down hard across the side of his head once and then again as the first impact threw him to the ground.

Blood spurted from his head onto his shoulder as he fell. He stretched out his arms as he hit the ground, then lay unmoving. Blood gushing from his ear, welling up from his scalp, matting his hair.

Diana dismounted and walked to where he lay, passing Sunny who stood frozen, still holding her shovel, staring at the man on the ground. My mother knelt beside him, looking at his face. His eyes were open and staring. She touched his throat and raised her head, looking up at us, the ones who watched.

She stood again. "We'll take him back," she said, "and bury him."

XIX

For two weeks after Bennett's death, Donna refused to leave her house, eating only enough to keep alive, isolating herself completely from the life of the village. When she did finally emerge, we were relieved, but that didn't last long. We soon began to dread the sight of her, dressed completely in black, her face cold and pale, her movements slow and deliberate. Although she walked through the village and ate at the dining hall and worked sometimes, she still would not speak to any of us or acknowledge us when we spoke to her. We could not laugh in her presence.

The day he died, we took his body from the woods slung across the back of a horse. Donna met us at the stream, half crawling up the bank. She was trembling with exhaustion, with fear, and with the physical pain of her dash from the village, alone, slower than the rest of us. It occurred to me to try to shield her from the sight of him, but I didn't move quickly enough. She approached him and, not touching, looked questioningly at Diana.

"He's dead, Donna," my mother said.

The young woman closed her eyes and clasped her hands into a single fist over her visibly pregnant stomach. Athena went to her and put her arm around her shoulder, steadying her, but Donna turned her face away and carefully, gently, removed Athena's arm. She sat down heavily and wrapped her arms around her head. She tried to bring her knees up, to roll herself into a ball, but her swollen stomach would not allow her to close herself up completely. Redwood strode to her, took off her own shirt, and kneeling, wrapped it around Donna. Then she picked her up and put her in the wagon. We took her back to her house. Redwood offered to stay with her for a while, and Angel went home to prepare what she called "remedies for grief."

Later that evening, I went with Athena to see how Donna was doing. There was no light, and no answer after my first knock. Frightened, I pounded on the door.

Angel opened it, blinking and rubbing her eyes. "She fell asleep, so I did too," she said sheepishly. I peered in. Donna was turning over in her bed, looking at us.

"Go away. All of you."

Relieved to hear her speak, I asked if there was anything we could do.

"Yes. You can bring me some black dye. And then go away."

Athena was puzzled. "Why do you want black dye?" Donna didn't answer. I said we would do as she asked. We both apologized for waking her.

"What does she want it for?" Athena asked again as we stepped out the door. I explained, as we walked to the clothing factory, that a long time ago people used to mourn their dead by wearing black.

"That must be the reason," I said. "I can't imagine what else she would want it for."

"That's good then, isn't it? She wouldn't be worrying about dyeing her clothes if she were planning to do herself any harm or try to run away. Don't you think?" She gave me no time to answer. "If she's going to dye her clothes black, that's quite a project. She must mean to wear them."

I nodded. "You're probably right. But we can't be sure. I wish I could feel that there's something we can do, some way to comfort her."

"Comfort from us? We killed him, Morgan."

We found the dye and went on to the dining hall to get some food for Donna and for Angel. As far as we knew, neither of them had eaten. Sara and Redwood were still sitting at one of the tables, talking.

Sara looked up when we came in. "What's the dye for?"

"It's for Donna," Athena said. "She wants to wear black."

Redwood frowned. "How is she?"

I shrugged. "She was sleeping at least, until we woke her up by banging on the door. She acts like she wants to be left alone. If one of us said that—but who knows what that means with Donna?"

Redwood chewed her thumbnail and looked at Sara, who murmured, "I don't know."

Athena spoke up. "Maybe she does want to be alone, but she isn't strong. I don't trust her. I'm going to stay with her tonight. I'm going to send Angel home and spend the night."

We returned to Donna's house with the food and the dye, and Angel let us in.

"Go on home, Angel. I'll stay with her," Athena said. "All of you go home."

"We can't do that, Donna," Athena said. "You need to have someone with you."

"Don't worry," Donna snapped. "I'm not going to try

to run away. Has he been buried yet?" The question was abrupt.

"I thought you gave her a sedative," I said to Angel.

"There's more." She pointed to a teapot sitting next to a burner on the stove—a stove that dominated one entire corner of the one-room house.

Athena was explaining that Bennett had been buried immediately, and that Diana, Sunny, and Calliope had done it. She repeated her demand to be allowed to stay in the house. "I won't bother you. I won't even talk to you if you don't want me to. I'll stay out of your way, even out of your sight—" she looked around at the one room— "if that's possible. I just want to help you. Please."

Donna lay back and closed her eyes. "All right. But you can't help me. And just you. No one else. I don't want to see anyone else."

I decided to say what I'd been thinking. "Look, Donna, he wasn't going to come back for you. He'd have needed help for that. Where would a runaway get help?" She stared at me blankly. Athena pushed me out the door.

Although Athena spent most of her nights watching over Donna, I saw her every day, and she kept me informed of Donna's mood and condition. Donna would not leave the house. For the first three days, she refused to eat at all, and then she began to eat small amounts, grudgingly. She spoke to Athena only rarely, and only when speech was absolutely necessary.

"She seems to be all right, really," Athena told me during one of our rare evenings together. "I talk to her, even though she doesn't answer me most of the time. It isn't that she acts angry toward me. It's more general than that. She just sits there brooding. I think a lot of it has to do with her child."

The child. According to Donna's calculations, it was due in less than three months. "What has she said about it? The child?"

"Oh, I was trying to get her to eat, and I said, 'You need to stay strong. You're carrying a child.' She just looked at me, in that new way she has, frantic and angry and bewildered all at once. And she said 'What if it's a boy? You know yours will be a girl. They always are. But mine—' She knows about the flower, Morgan. She asked me if she could eat one now, if that would help."

"She probably overheard someone, a child maybe. We've all felt freer with Bennett dead. We shouldn't, I suppose. And when you told her it wouldn't help?"

"She said, 'I'll kill him myself. I won't let you do it.' "

I shuddered. I felt sick and irritated at the same time. "There's at least as good a chance that it will be a girl." But I was thinking, it just goes on and on. We can't get away from it. "Anyway, you don't need to be worrying about that now. Think of yourself and your own child." They mattered to me, Athena and her child. A great deal. "You look exhausted. Maybe it's time you stopped babysitting with Donna."

"I suppose I am tired. I'm worried about her, worried about her baby. And the women who'll be leaving. I can't remember ever having so much to worry about before."

I stood up. "There never has been so much to worry about before. We don't know what to do with it all. Maybe Sunny's right. Maybe we need more challenges. Maybe we've gotten weak." I took her hand and began to lead her out of the room. "Maybe we should go to bed."

She held back. "More challenges? More misery, you mean. I don't need it. But babysitting—Morgan, you shouldn't say that. She's not a baby. She's had a terrible loss. If I could only reassure her, but I can't. All I can do is spend time with her for a while." She began to walk with me, but slowly. "Maybe just a few more days. I have to see some kind of change. If she'd talk more, or eat more, or if she'd leave the house, start living in the village again. It wouldn't take much. Some little thing. Anything."

"All right." I regretted my use of the term. "I understand. Not babysitting. But the responsibility isn't just yours." We sat down together on the bed. I held her and stroked her back. "I'm concerned about you. If she has to deal with someone besides you, maybe she'll agree to. And you'll get some rest."

"But I like her. Sweetheart, her family sold her. We never accepted her as one of us. The only time she belonged anywhere was when she belonged to someone—Bennett. We haven't given her anything. We've taken away everything she had, and she doesn't even have a place to have her baby. Safely."

I pulled back from her and cupped my hands around her face. "We're not going to kill a baby. We're not." She only looked at me, doubting, mirroring my own doubt. "And we can't give her a place to be safe. She has to take it. Take it from us. With us. And she may not be able to."

We held each other again, and we went to bed, and we managed eventually to sleep in the comfort of each other.

I was too busy during the day to think much about Donna. The job Sara had asked me to do for the new settlement, the copying of the records, was a massive one. It was disturbing, too. Working on it so many hours a day, directing others in their work, gave me a strange, uncomfortable feeling. As though my life, all our lives, were dead inscriptions on an ancient tablet. For the first time, it occurred to me that life in the new village might eventually be quite different from that which had developed in ours. Even in Demeter, the old peaceful days were gone. Bennett was dead, but the effects of his coming were still with us. Our new knowledge of the world had changed us. The discovery that there had been another village like ours and that some of its women might still be alive was creating wild speculation and even wilder plans for the future. Redwood was pushing for a high birth rate, and Angel accused her of wanting to build an army. She didn't deny it.

I'd been working at the copying for more than two weeks when Donna came out of her house. I had been taking a short break from my desk, standing on the doorstep trying to clear my mind and stretch my muscles, looking at the green hills, when I saw Athena and Donna strolling through town, Donna in a long, clumsy black garment of her own making. I saw several passersby stop and try to speak to her, but she only shook her head and turned her face away from them.

Later that day when Athena came to spend some time with me and help me with the copying, she said Donna had eaten breakfast that morning in the dining hall, "a real breakfast."

"Is she talking to you more than she was?"

"Yes. Mostly about her family."

"She can't go back to them," I said quickly.

Athena glared at me. "She knows that." I was sure she thought I was unsympathetic on the subject of Donna, and I supposed I was. I didn't feel terribly proud of myself for my attitude; I just didn't have the energy to give. "Besides," Athena continued, "I don't think she wants to go back to them. Why should she?"

I handed her another book of records with pages marked for copying. "Has she mentioned Bennett at all?"

"Only indirectly. She said we were a village of murderers." Athena sat down at a small table placed near my desk and began to work.

I thought about what Donna had said to her: a village of murderers. There were some in the town who might agree with her, and it was true, in a way. But I had done some soul-searching of my own and concluded that we needed to feel no collective guilt for protecting ourselves from betrayal and destruction. I refused to dwell on it, to worry about it. What was, was. Still, I didn't want Athena to think me unfeeling. I cared that she thought well of me. I looked over at her, working, and decided to interrupt her, to talk a little more about Donna. Besides, I had an idea.

"Athena?" She looked up. "Will she talk to anyone besides you?"

"Not yet."

"I've been thinking. All these records, all this history —it might help us to help her." Athena looked interested. "We could make her understand what happened and why it happened. She needs to know. It would be good for her to know."

"How would we go about it?"

"We could teach her. We could take some time with her. All she knows about us, about Demeter, she's picked up by accident. She already knows about us. She knows we're here, and she knows about the flower. What else do we have to hide?"

Athena was nodding, eager to hear more.

"We could teach her about the founding, make her understand, make her part of it."

Athena smiled at me, but she looked doubtful. "I don't know how much of that I can do. But maybe if you help me And Angel . . ."

I spoke to Angel about it at dinner. She liked the idea and agreed to help, if she could. "We should have done it sooner."

Diana looked offended. "We couldn't. There was Bennett. And we haven't just ignored her after all."

"She needs to see the records for herself," I said. "She needs to read them and have someone to talk to about them, to answer her questions."

"There's a problem with that," Diana replied. "She can't read."

I'd never known anyone who couldn't read. It hadn't occurred to me that such a thing was possible. But then I hadn't really bothered to think about her education or lack of it.

"In that case," I said, "we'll have to teach her to read."

Late that night, I was sitting at my desk looking through the chronicles, thinking about Donna being able to read them, when I heard a knock on the half-open door.

"Come in," I said and turned to see Sunny walk in. I had seen her only in passing, at meals and around the village, since the day of Bennett's death. I knew that she was busy getting ready to leave so I hadn't wondered very much at her solemn, detached, almost unfriendly attitude. But I noticed again how pale and weary she looked.

"Hi, Morgan." She pulled up an extra chair and sat next to me, her elbow on my desk.

"Hi, Sunny. How are you?"

"All right. I was just talking to Athena about Donna." I nodded, waiting for her to go on. She was looking down at the floor. "I think I should try to talk to her."

"Why? Why should you?"

"Because I killed him. She's blaming the whole village, and I'm the one who killed him."

I stared at her. "Sunny, the village *did* kill him. She's right. Have you been carrying the whole weight of it all this time?" She wouldn't look at me and didn't answer. "Sunny! That's crazy. There's no need for you to feel personally responsible, to feel guilty."

"If I'm not guilty, who is?"

"You know better than that. You know it was inevitable, just because of the way things are—"

"And I was just an instrument of fate," she retorted. "What idiocy. The point is, inevitable or not, necessary or not, I killed him. I may adjust to the idea eventually. I expect I'll have to kill someone else someday. But before I leave the village I'm going to tell Donna that I was the one. I've got to take her anger and whatever else she needs to give me and take it out of here with me."

I stood and went to her, putting my arms around her, holding her head against me. "You want her to punish you?"

"Yes."

"Then go and talk to her." I felt her nod in answer before she pulled away from me. She left immediately. I worked until I was too sleepy to work any more and went home to bed.

Athena and I met for breakfast the following morning. I brought with me some of the notes I'd made the night before on Donna's course of study. Athena was waiting for me when I arrived, sitting at a table with Ocean, Calliope, and Firstborn. Sara, one of those cooking that morning, advised me against the cereal, saying it was "gluey." I took eggs and toast and went to my table.

"How's the cereal?" I asked Calliope, who was spooning it into her mouth with obvious hungry pleasure.

"Gluey," she said grinning. "Just the way I like it."

I sat close to Athena and handed her the notes. She took them, glanced through them, and put them aside.

"Sunny came to see Donna last night," she said.

"Yes. I know. What happened?"

"It was strange. Hard to describe." Calliope and Ocean had stopped eating to listen. Firstborn continued to eat. "It was so sad. Sunny didn't even come in. She knocked and I opened the door and she said she wanted to see Donna. So Donna came to the door. Sunny told her that she was the one who killed Bennett. Donna just stared at her for a long time and then she began to cry."

"That's all?" Ocean wanted to know.

"She just cried. And Sunny stood there looking at her, saying, 'Aren't you going to say anything to me? I killed him.' And she said, 'The village didn't do it. I did.' And Donna kept on crying, and then Sunny began to cry. And I cried too. Then Sunny left. I saw her this morning. I think she feels better. She even smiled at me, in a sickly kind of way."

Firstborn was nodding thoughtfully. "Well, it certainly is true, you know. Sunny did kill him. I certainly don't feel that I did." I heard Athena sigh, softly, at her mother's words.

"And how's Donna?" Ocean asked, ignoring First-born.

"I thought we'd start her lessons this afternoon," Athena said. "She seems interested enough. But what Sunny told her—it hasn't made much difference that I can see. She still blames us. All of us."

"Maybe that will change, with time," Calliope said.

Athena looked skeptical. "Maybe."

XX

The final organizing and rechecking of the copied records kept me frantically busy the week before the scheduled departure of the first wagon. I had to be sure that everything needed was included and that information about the flower and the location of Demeter was left out. We had to accept the possibility that the records and those who carried them might be captured on the way to the new village.

Our history was going with Sunny and Luna in the lead wagon. The other eight wagons would follow one at a time, at intervals, as the founders had done when they came to Demeter.

During that last week, Athena was quieter than usual. I knew she wanted me to suggest that we consider living together and sharing the birth of her daughter, but I was still unable to say the words. Too much of Sunny remained. As strong as my new feelings for Athena were, they were new. And Sunny was still in the village.

The night before the departure, I could not sleep. Athena dozed, woke to hold me and talk to me, and dozed again. I got up twice to drink tea, trying to clear my mind and make it empty so I could sleep. Finally, in the chilly dark just before dawn, I gave up, dressed, and built a small fire to warm Athena when she woke again. When the first thin light of the sun appeared, I began to hear voices outside and went to the window. Women were leaving their houses, assembling at the road, gathering for the dawn departure, waiting to say goodbye.

The sounds woke Athena before I could. She swallowed her tea quickly, and we headed toward Donna's house. She had told Athena that she wanted to be there and wanted to go with us.

Although I wouldn't have chosen to spend this morning in Donna's company, Athena had told her we would be happy to have her. I was in a precarious emotional state, jittery from lack of sleep, hungry but unable to eat. And here I was, I thought impatiently, waiting for Donna to drag herself out of bed and join us.

When she finally appeared, she was dressed in her usual bulbous black mourning dress. Wonderful, I thought. A cheerful last sight for the new settlers. A figure of doom on a now thoroughly depressing morning.

I scowled at Donna, and Athena, walking up behind me, pinched me hard on the bottom she so admired. Shocked, I stopped and stared at her. She looked back at me as if she were wondering what on earth I was staring at her for. I shook my head, trying not to laugh.

"Oh, all right," I said snappishly. I would try to behave.

Donna, waiting for us to catch up with her, didn't seem to have noticed either my scowl or our interchange.

The wagon was waiting, loaded and ready, outside the

door of Luna's house. Sunny had already taken the driver's seat. Luna was putting a last small box of what looked like personal possessions under a corner of the heavy, half unrolled cover. Diana was there, fussing over a bag of Demeter flower seeds, placing it carefully between two crates and lashing it down tight. Angel stood beside her giving her advice and testing the knot to be sure the seeds were secure.

Nearby, arm in arm, Redwood and Freedom watched. Freedom, who would herself be leaving in a few days, sharing a wagon with Sara and Joanna, looked excited and worried. Redwood just looked worried. I noticed she glanced at Freedom from time to time, covertly, the look of a mother who wanted to protect her child but knew that she couldn't. They seemed to be drawing closer to each other than they had been before, now that Freedom was going away.

Sara and Joanna came strolling down the road from their house as though there were nothing to be excited about, stopping to talk to friends, working their way gradually toward the loaded wagon. They nodded to us as they passed, and Donna looked after them, shaking her head in a half-admiring, half-dismayed manner.

"Are they really sixty years old?" she asked Athena.

"Joanna's sixty-five," I answered.

She shook her head again. It was good to see her showing wonder instead of her usual bleak bitterness. Maybe the lessons were helping. Angel had told me that Donna was learning to read quickly and seemed to enjoy it.

Sunny was still sitting in the driver's seat, leaning over to accept hugs and kisses of goodbye. Luna was talking importantly to Sara and Joanna. She had not yet climbed up beside Sunny. I made a quick decision.

"Athena?" She stepped closer to me. I squeezed her hand and gave her a loving and reassuring kiss. "I'll be right back." I worked my way through the crowd to the wagon and, not giving myself time to think, abruptly pulled myself up onto the seat.

Sunny pulled back from me slightly. "I wish you hadn't come, Morgan. I don't want to say goodbye to you. I had hoped that you would understand that." I nodded, yes, I had understood, but I had decided to say goodbye anyway. I had needed to come out before dawn to watch Sunny leave, and now I needed to be close enough to her to know that she was actually going.

"I don't want to say goodbye to you, either," I answered. With those words I could feel the tears starting, but I struggled successfully to hold them back. "So I won't say it." I groped in my pocket. "I only wanted to wish you luck and to give you this." I handed her a last brief chronicle entry to go with the volumes they were taking with them. I had written it and copied it during the sleepless night before in preparation for this morning. It told of their departure. "Maybe I'll come and visit you some time. Maybe Athena and I will come."

She took the entry from me and glanced at it, and I noticed as she reached behind her to put it safely in her pack that her eyes had filled with tears. When they overflowed, she brushed them away roughly. "Yes. And maybe I'll come back to see you and the others once we're settled. A hundred miles isn't very far, is it?" She had cut the figure by fifty miles, but I didn't correct her.

"No," I agreed. "It isn't very far at all."

We could not look directly at each other. She put her arms around me suddenly, impulsively, and we held each other. I felt all the old love, but it was different. It was something I couldn't have. I pulled free, and I think I succeeded in smiling at her before I jumped down to the ground. Athena came to stand beside me. Calliope and Ocean came too, and Donna hovered at the edge of our small group. The area immediately surrounding the wagon was now completely usurped by those who would be going in the succeeding days, tense, excited, engaging in last-minute consultations with the lead group. I realized that I had been staring at Sunny's back and looked away.

"Morgan?" Calliope was speaking to me. I looked at her brightly, and she frowned at my falseness. "Morgan, I don't think we need to stand here and watch them go, do you?"

"Let's go to my house," Athena said. "I'll make breakfast, just for the five of us."

Ocean nodded rapidly. "Good idea. I'll get some food from the dining hall."

I shook my head. "I don't want to go yet. It's exciting." And it was. The crowd, the anticipation of adventure, of history about to be made—I stood outside it, watching, trying to share the high, expectant mood. Diana and Angel were holding hands, and Sara and Joanna had ended their conversation with the other new settlers and had gone to stand with their old friends. Freedom once again was close by Redwood's side. Luna unrolled the wagon cover, tying it down at the corners. She vaulted up onto the seat next to Sunny. The women nearest the wagon stepped back. Sunny waved goodbye and, her arm still raised but her attention fully on the horses, began to guide the wagon down the road.

"Come on, Morgan." Athena was touching my arm. "Let's go back."

Diana, Angel, Sara, and Joanna were walking toward us, amid the dispersing crowd.

"Good morning, Mother," I said.

"Good morning, Morgan," Diana answered warmly, nodding in a smiling but distracted way toward my friends. The four elders walked near us, but not with us, intent only on each other, and I heard my mother say, "Well, after all, we traveled a lot farther than that to get here."

Angel laughed. "Maybe so, but they've still got good

reason to be terrified, just like we were."

"Terrified?" Sara said indignantly.

"And we didn't have a mother village to help us, either," Diana persisted. I glanced at her in time to see a teasing smile brush across her lips. Joanna was grinning.

"Listen here, Diana," Sara said loudly. "We're not terrified and we don't need your damned help, either. Sunny and I . . ."

We could still hear the elders laughing when we reached Athena's door.